BLOOD AND SAND

THE LACROIX MYSTERIES

COURTNEY DEAN

CHAPTER ONE

DETECTIVE REY LACROIX

LOUISIANA

Three years later...

"Baby, your phone's ringing."

Groaning, I rolled over after removing Chanel's naked body from my chest and squinted, trying to read the red numbers on the alarm clock sitting on the nightstand through blurred vision.

Fucking five-thirty in the morning.

I gripped the sides of my head; the pounding felt like my brain was banging against my skull. It had been a long night. This was one hell of a hangover I'd have to deal with.

After working a long shift, instead of taking my ass home like I should have to start my long weekend of wallowing in misery, I decided to go to *Lucky's Dive*, the local watering hole. I'd needed to drink myself into oblivion before calling Chanel to come over and fuck away my dreaded existence in the house I'd once shared with *her*.

This had been my routine for the past three years. Nothing was the same since she decided to walk out of my life, and I decided not to fight for her. My mother always said my stubborn ways would cost me something important one day, and they had.

It cost me everything.

It cost me her.

I couldn't even say her name. It hurt too much, like my heart was being squeezed in a vise. I really shouldn't have been pissed she walked away from our marriage for her dream job. She'd worked hard to achieve it. But I was pissed.

Well, not pissed, just hurt. We promised each other forever. Now I was alone, and she was moving forward without me.

I fumbled around for my ringing cell phone in the pitch-black room. At this time of the morning, it couldn't be anything good.

"LaCroix."

"Head down to Laurels Bayou." Captain Broussard's voice sounded through the hangover clouding my mind. "We got two more floaters."

"But Cap," I ran my hands through my hair, frustrated, exhausted, and hungover, "I'm off until Tuesday night. Can't you call Shaw?"

Two more hours of sleep was all I'd be able to get before I needed to be on the road. He'd just interrupted the little time I had left to sleep off this hangover, and it was my day off.

I shoulda brought my ass home instead of going to Lucky's.

Around this time of the year, I picked up as many extra shifts as possible before taking a very long weekend. This year was no different than the last two. I worked to the point of exhaustion, drank until I couldn't function, and fucked until I forgot about her, at least for a little while. I'd planned to drown my sorrows away this weekend while I took my boat out on the lake, fished, and mourned the love of my life in privacy, for the third year in a row. It had become my ritual. My time of regret. Being drunk and alone was my penance for being an asshole.

The happiest day of my life occurred this month, three years ago. Our wedding day. This month also marked the worst day of my life, the day she left me—two weeks before our anniversary.

"Well, LaCroix, if you no longer want to be the lead on this investigation so you can wallow in self-pity about your fuck up, I'll hand the files over to Rankin, and he can take over as lead detective."

My jaw clenched. If I could've reached through the phone and choked the life out of him, I would have been a happy man. He knew this was the only weekend I requested off all year, and to threaten to take my case away from me was a low blow. Rankin was a newbie and couldn't distinguish his head from his ass if he had to, much less solve multiple murders. He only had the job because his father was the former sheriff. Cap knew I would never let my case be handed to someone else, especially to someone like Rankin. I owed it to all the families of these murdered women to find out what happened to them.

"No, sir." I sighed. "I can be there in an hour."

"Make it thirty, LaCroix," he ordered, ending the call without waiting for my response.

"Son of a bitch!" I rose from the bed naked, phone clenched tightly in hand. If I hadn't needed it, I would have thrown the shit across the room. "Get up, Chanel. You got to head home. I've been called in."

"Why can't I just stay until you get back, baby?" she asked, groaning. "You fucked me good last night. I'm tired. I just need to sleep a little longer."

Chanel and I had known each other since high school, and we hooked up on occasion. But when I met my ex-wife, our on-again-off-again sexual relationship ended. It was no secret that Chanel hated Dana for tying me down. For unknown reasons, the woman believed we were high school sweethearts and would eventually marry. We were not high school sweethearts, and I would never marry her. Let's just say, she was the only one who was thrilled when Dana and I divorced.

Same as in high school, we slipped back into our old routine—I'd get drunk, call her so we could fuck, then I'd leave, or she'd leave, depending on the situation. That was the extent of our non-relationship, and there was no way in hell I would let Chanel stay in my house when I wasn't there. We didn't have that type of connection, and we never would.

I ignored her use of the term of endearment the first time, but I couldn't let it slide anymore. Every time she used it, I inwardly cringed, and I'd told her constantly not to say it. She wasn't my girl, my woman, nor my wife, so I sure as hell wasn't her baby.

"Don't call me that." I didn't wait for her response because she'd play ignorant. She always did. "We've already had this talk, Chanel. Don't call me that shit, and you're not staying here. *Ever.*"

"Why?" she asked, her eyes narrowing. "It's because of *her,* isn't it?"

Yes, it's because of her, was what I should have said, but I didn't owe Chanel or anyone else an explanation for what happened inside my own damn house. I picked up her clothes from the floor and tossed them at her. "Get dressed and be gone before I get out of the shower."

I stalked across the hall to my master bedroom to shower away the stench of alcohol and sex, slammed the bedroom door behind me, then locked it. I didn't need Chanel anywhere near *our* space. It was bad enough I'd allowed her into *our* home. I would wait for the guilt to swamp me after Chanel left.

No matter how long it had been since Dana left, I'd never been able to have another woman step foot in the bedroom we shared. Until a few months ago, Chanel hadn't even been allowed to step foot in my house, and I only allowed it now because I got tired of dishing out money for cheap hotel rooms when I had a perfectly good spare bedroom with a decent bed I could use for free.

By the time I stepped out of the shower, Chanel was long gone, and once again, I was in my house alone. At times, it was depressing, mostly around this time of year. Everything reminded me of DeeDee. I refused to change a single thing, keeping it just how she left it, from the same furniture to the pictures on the walls. It was the only thing that kept her in my life. Other times, I worked so much, I didn't have time to dwell on it.

I constantly replayed our last time together like a film flickering through my mind. I'd watched her hold back tears and pack her bags while my stubborn ass smugly looked on, daring her to leave me.

She showed my ass.

When I didn't call within her requested time frame, the divorce papers were served the following week, stating irreconcilable differences. Although I'd wanted to fight for our marriage, I'd remained steadfast in my decision. I couldn't uproot my life for her because of my job.

Selfish, I know.

So, she started her new journey without me.

It was the biggest mistake I'd ever made. A mistake I was still paying for.

I looked down at the gold wedding ring on my finger and twisted the thick yellow band. After three years, I still couldn't bring myself to take it off. If I did, it was admitting we were truly over. I still couldn't let go.

I shook my head. "Get your head out of your ass, LaCroix," I berated myself for dwelling on shit I couldn't change. "You got murders to solve. No time for a pity party now. You made your decision. She's gone. Now, fucking live with it."

I dressed quickly, secured my sidearm to my waist, and then downed four aspirins with Jameson from the bottle sitting on my nightstand. After I snatched up my keys and phone, I rushed out the door.

Chapter Two

Detective Rey LaCroix

Laurels Bayou

Arriving at the crime scene with only minutes to spare, I pulled off to the side of the two-lane rural road just in time to see the sun peeking over the horizon. To keep the area as secure as possible, the crime scene had been cordoned off with squad cars and yellow caution tape, and portable blue screens had been erected, but their true function was to shield the bodies being pulled from the dark water from the media.

The local media were like vultures. They'd already gotten wind of the two new bodies that had been discovered floating in the murky waters of Laurels Bayou, and they'd descended on the area like flies attracted to shit. These bodies represented the tenth and eleventh to be pulled out of this same bayou in the past eight months.

I exited my truck and pushed my way through the growing crowd of reporters shouting questions and their cameramen.

"Detective LaCroix, is there a serial killer in Louisiana targeting Black women?" Stacy Benoit, a reporter for WTEA-Louisiana, yelled, sticking a microphone in my face. She gave me that smile she always plastered on her face whenever she saw me. The "if you tell me what you know, I will make it worth your time" smile. I wasn't falling for that shit again.

Stacy and I had spent a night or two together after my divorce, but I cut her off quickly after I discovered that she'd sucked my dick for an anonymous source within the police department rather than us enjoying great food and sex.

I pushed the microphone away without answering her question. Even though it was Stacy, I wanted to scream, "Hell yes, there is a serial killer targeting Black women in Louisiana," to issue a warning for women to be on guard. However, I knew they'd force me off the case if I responded. So, I remained quiet. It was better to be on the case than not.

"Detective LaCroix, do you have any suspects?" another reporter I didn't recognize yelled. He looked as though he was fresh out of high school and wasn't old enough to be at a crime scene. I refused to answer his question as well.

But the answer was fuck no. Despite the increasing number of victims filling the morgue, we didn't have any suspects. Regardless of the eyes we had on this killing field, whoever the murderer was, he came and went as he pleased, dropping bodies along the way.

"Can you give us something, Detective LaCroix?" the young reporter continued. "Women are dying, specifically Black women. What are the police doing to stop these murders?"

I pushed my way through the crowd, not answering any questions. I had no information to give, and what I could share, the department was keeping a lid on. While the sounds of reporters' questions and news helicopters circling overheard pierced my ears, I forced myself to block them all out and focus on the task at hand. Catching a psycho killer.

Hanging my badge around my neck, I slid between a couple of squad cars blocking off the highway, ducked under the caution tape, and passed the patrol officers standing guard to keep prying eyes from disturbing the scene.

The stale, swampy aroma of the bayou wafted in the air. The humidity was already extremely high despite the early morning hour. Mosquitos the size of fucking golf balls and gnats were already relentless. The weight of the hot, moist air caused my powder blue polo shirt to stick to my body, forcing me to put my shoulder-length hair into a bun. Temperatures were already in the upper seventies, and the high today was supposed to be closer to one-hundred degrees. With the combination of the sweltering heat and a massive fucking hangover, this was the start of my long weekend...defin itely not the long weekend I'd had planned.

I walked over to the edge of the bayou, where a few detectives from the homicide division milled around, waiting for the bodies to be pulled from the water. Although we already had over fifty homicides this year because we were in the middle of a gang war, everyone was hands on deck anytime the bodies were pulled from Laurels Bayou, which I appreciated.

"I thought you were leaving for the lake this morning?" Shaw asked.

Amir Shaw had been my partner for the last six years while in homicide. We'd been through a lot, on and off the job, including my divorce. There were times he'd pulled me out of *Lucky's* drunk off my ass, and I'd done the same for him before he finally got his shit together and married his wife. Now, he had the picture-perfect family. He was a cookie-cutter husband and father with the white picket fence and a beautiful daughter. Shaw wasn't only my partner—he was my best friend. We'd become so close that he and his wife, Delaney, had asked DeeDee and me to be the godparents to their only child.

"*Nope*. Cap threatened to pull me off the case and give it to Rankin if I didn't get my ass down here. So here I am, and my weekend is gone to shit. But hey, at least I can work until I drop dead to forget about the next few days, huh?" I waved away the gnats flying in my face and chuckled, trying to mask the pain I drowned in, but my friend saw through it. He always did.

We did this same song and dance every year. My piss-poor attitude wasn't a surprise to him.

"Man, Delaney's worried about you," Amir said. "You haven't been by to see Amara in a while, and you know how she feels about you fucking Chanel."

I only nodded because there was nothing to say. I know they worried, but nothing could change my life. Not now.

"I'm not trying to be in your business like that," he continued, "but your sex life is causing problems in my marriage." He crossed his arms over his chest and laughed before his face turned serious again. "But I'll give you a pass because I know how hard this time of the year is for you."

"Well, tell Delaney there's no need to worry, and there's no need for you to worry, either. I'm good," I assured, despite it being a lie. "Now tell me, what do we have?"

I tried to shift the conversation away from my misery to what was important. Our investigation. It was time for us to get to work on this case and not dwell on my life or lack thereof. Besides, I already knew what Amir would say. It was the same thing he and Delaney had been saying since the divorce. I needed to stop beating myself up over the decision I'd made. It was done and over with. I shouldn't spiral out of control over it. But neither of them understood. How could they? They had each other, and all I had was the fucking job I gave my other half up for, a piece of ass I couldn't care less about, and a bottle of Jameson waiting for me in my fucking empty house. I was no longer Rey LaCroix, husband of the most spectacular woman on the planet. I was a shell of a man now that she was gone.

"We have two females intricately bound with rope," Shaw said, bringing me back to my miserable reality. There was no time to dwell on my fuck up; it was done and over with. Had been for three years. Now, we had two more dead girls floating in the bayou.

"Just like the others?" I asked, even though I already knew the answer. This was his killing field. His territory. Of course, it was just like the others. Black women, bound, murdered, and discarded like trash.

"It seems so. We'll know more once they're on the slab at the morgue. But seems to be the same type of rope, and the bodies were linked together, like the others."

"But why discard them in twos?" I spoke more to myself than Shaw, but he nodded in agreement. "And why bind them so intricately? I've never seen anything like it."

It was the same question I'd asked myself since we recovered the first two bodies no less than thirty yards from this exact location. There had to be a reason to go through such efforts to bind these women this way. "There has to be a reason for everything he's doing. What are their connections to one another?"

"Like the others, they're both African American females, possibly in their mid-twenties to mid-thirties, dark hair, no visible tattoos. Also, each body has been stripped of clothing, no jewelry present, intricately bound with rope."

No matter what Cap said, we had a serial killer on our hands attacking young Black women in Louisiana, and he fucking knew it. Why the hell deny it?

"Who called it in?"

Shaw pulled a small black notebook from his back pocket and began flipping through the pages. "Let's see. A... Mr. Gary Sutton, thirty-four-year-old, White male and divorced father of two. Originally from North Carolina but moved to Louisiana around seven years ago. Says he was out fishing and stumbled upon the bodies floating in the water. He's waiting for us back at the station."

"All right. Anything else?"

"Have you thought about what I asked you?"

I groaned, rubbing my temples.

"You know she can help with this, Rey."

This wasn't a good conversation to have if I wanted my skull to stop feeling like a jackhammer was beating down on it. Shaw had been on my ass since we pulled bodies number three and four out of the water for me to contact Dana for insight on the case. We both knew this guy was a different beast, and we needed the help. Specifically, her help. So far, I hadn't been able to push myself to do it. How do I face the woman who still had my heart after I didn't fight for us?

Although Dana was still in contact with Amir and Delaney, they never gave me any information about what she'd been up to, and I never asked. I didn't want to make our friends uncomfortable. Everything I did know about my ex-wife and her new life came from news reports or social media. She'd done well for herself since she left me. Somehow, I couldn't bring myself to disrupt what she had built for herself. However, Amir was right. She could help. She was the best at what she did.

"No, I haven't," I finally confessed.

"Rey…"

I threw up my hand, stopping his protest. "I know, Amir, but I can't call her out of the fucking blue about a case. I haven't talked to her since the night I stood there like a fucking idiot while she left me. Even during the divorce proceedings, she didn't want to speak to me. What makes you think she would even see me?"

"Because it's DeeDee, man," he said, like I was the dumbest person on Earth. "Just go to Atlanta so she can do that crazy shit she does. You remember how many cases she helped us solve while she was in school. We need her help, Rey. There's no other way. We've never dealt with anything like this."

"So, you want me to just show up at her job out of the blue? You think after three years, she'll see me?"

"Regardless of what you think, Rey, you were the center of DeeDee's world, and no matter how much you hurt her with your decision, if she would see anyone out of the blue, it would be you. I have no doubt she would help, but I think you should be the one to ask her. Not me."

"I'll think about it."

"Don't think about it—do it before he drops two more on us."

Contacting Dana would be hard, and I wasn't sure I was ready to face her, even after three years.

"We'll go talk with the guy who found the bodies, and hopefully, we can identify these women and notify the families before the media gets wind of who they are." Not only had solving these cases become my life's work, but identifying these missing women and returning them to their families had also become my mission. I wanted the families to have the opportunity to say their proper goodbyes and not think about their loved ones' last days.

We walked over to the water's edge, where the stench of death intermingled with briny algae and the decay of rotting dead trees. I had gotten used to the smell of death and the bayou. I'd been around death for years as a homicide detective and grew up on the bayou, but the mixture of the two would have most upchucking their lunch.

The divers gently removed the two bodies from the water, carefully placing them on two orange basket stretchers that had been latched together to push them out of the water onto the bank of the bayou. Rotting vegetation and scummy water covered their lifeless grayish skin while white clouded eyes stared back at us.

Fucking eerie and heartbreaking at the same time.

"I'm not one for hating people, but damn I hate this guy," Amir muttered when Dr. Nguyen, the medical examiner, zipped the black body bags.

"Me and you both," I said.

We walked back toward the throng of media personnel barricaded behind squad cars, ignoring their questions. The coroner's office placed both bodies in the back of the van to head to the morgue.

"You riding with me?" I asked Shaw.

"Nah, I'll meet you there."

I nodded and jumped in my truck, headed to the police station to see what information I could gather from the man who'd found the bodies. Then, I would work to identify these murdered women.

Well, if I can't drink my misery away, at least I can work through it.

CHAPTER THREE

DR. DANA LaCROIX

ATLANTA

It had been three years since I accepted my dream job in Atlanta, and despite all the accolades, awards, and accomplishments, a part of me was still missing. I knew why and who caused the feeling, and I still hadn't been able to push the asshole from my heart completely. Now, lying here in another man's arms, a man I should give my all to and move forward , I couldn't.

"Your mind is working overtime, Dana."

Aaron pulled my naked frame closer to his muscular body. The warmth from his skin caused me to snuggle closer. He ran his fingers through my kinky hair, massaging my scalp. I groaned and closed my eyes, surrendering to the feeling of being in Aaron's arms and not Rey's, if just for this moment.

"You want to talk about it?"

His deep, gruff voice brought an awareness to what my reality truly was. I was no longer married. I held tighter to Aaron while I tried to push thoughts of Rey out of my mind. Aaron had a crazy way of reading me, especially when my thoughts strayed to Rey. I didn't know if a look showed on my face that he'd learned to recognize, but when it happened, he had no problem calling me out on it.

Aaron's here, not my ex-husband, and this isn't a conversation I want to have.

FBI Special Agent Aaron Hart had been my on-again, off-again boyfriend since my divorce was finalized three years ago. With both of us having grueling schedules, it was hard to have a meaningful relationship, but we clung to each other anyway after we'd gone through our divorces around the same time. We understood the ache of losing someone we'd hoped to spend the rest of our lives with due to our careers, and we'd connected with one another through that experience.

Although, right now, we were in our off-again stage, I had a tough time turning down an explosive night of sex with him, especially when there was a tough case, and I needed to relieve stress. I assumed he came to me for the same reason since he was the one who'd asked for time apart.

At first, I had reservations about getting involved with him so quickly after my divorce. We were colleagues, and I wasn't completely over Rey, even if I was the one to start the divorce proceedings. But after learning Rey had moved on with no other than Chanel Boudreaux before the ink had even dried on our divorce papers, I let my reservations go.

Only a couple of months after our divorce was finalized, I returned to Louisiana to see my goddaughter, and Chanel had been more than happy to divulge her relationship with my ex-husband after we ran into each other at a local department store. It had taken everything in me not to throttle the woman, but what would be the point? Rey had made his decision, and he didn't choose me.

If Rey could move on, why couldn't I?

Aaron was a girl's dream—caring, attentive, and could cook as good as a Michelin Star chef, not to mention his massages were to die for. To top it all off, he was gorgeous. Dark skin, dark eyes, a muscular build, thick lips, and perfect white teeth. Aaron Hart was *the* perfect package, in bed and out. However, he had one strike against him when it came to me—he wasn't Rey LaCroix, and that was the one thing I couldn't get past, no matter how hard I tried.

Aaron was the total opposite of Rey, instantly attracting me to him, from his healthy eating habits to his mellow attitude. Rey went to the gym only to work off the cheeseburgers and Cajun food he loved to scarf down, and he was an asshole most of the time. Aaron was what I needed, someone to wipe Rey completely out of my mind and heart. However, Aaron had continually brought up the topic of marriage last year, and the more he brought it up, the more I pulled away.

It wasn't like he wasn't husband material. Any lady would be lucky to have him as a husband, including me. He just wasn't *my* husband...well, my ex-husband. And until I purged Rey LaCroix from my system completely, neither Aaron nor anyone else would have a place in my heart. I cared for Aaron, but my love, I feared, would always be Rey's.

How pathetic is that?

"You're thinking about him *again*, aren't you?"

I heard the agitation in his voice, but there wasn't anything I could do about it. Rey was a touchy subject, one that wasn't going away.

"Let's not do this right now, Aaron. I've got a million and one things to take care of at the office before I head to my grandparents." He was right. I was thinking of Rey, but I wouldn't admit to it.

I got out of my bed and headed to the bathroom, trying to avoid the conversation.

"Stop running, Dana."

"I'm not running, Aaron."

"Yes, you are!" He sat up in the bed, the sheet falling to his waist. My eyes zoomed in on his hairless skin. He looked like he was sculpted from stone.

"We're going to have to talk about him sometime so we can move forward. Together. I want to marry you. I love you."

But I don't love you.

"I can't and won't play second to anyone, not even your ex."

"I've never asked you to play second to anyone!" I took a deep breath and released it. "Now is not the time to discuss any of this, Aaron."

"Well, when would be the right time, Dana?" he asked, his tone causing me to flinch. "We've been together for three damn years. I'm ready to move forward."

But I'm not. Just say it.

"I'm not getting into this with you." I took the coward's way out. I cared for Aaron. I wasn't trying to hurt him. "Discussing my ex-husband is off limits."

I slammed the bathroom door. I knew what he wanted to say. This was a recurring discussion and argument, but now was not the time. I needed to get ready for the start of my workday and then get on a plane to North Carolina for my vacation. Hopefully, by the time I finished my shower, Aaron would be gone, and I could avoid the elephant in the room—Rey LaCroix.

• • • ● • ● • • • •

ATLANTA FIELD OFFICE

Placing my purse and messenger bag on the conveyor belt, I waited in the employees' line for my turn to pass through the metal detectors right outside the restricted area of my office building. With my stainless-steel cup in hand filled with my morning cappuccino, there were only a few minutes to spare before the briefing with Mr. Steele, the Special Agent-in-Charge, on an important case he assigned to me. The disappearance of six-year-old Whitney Harry.

It had taken me hours to sift through the local detective's case files, including crime scene photos and witness statements, before I came up with a workable profile of the unsub in the short amount of time he'd requested. It had been very nerve-wracking and stressful, hence my night and morning full of stress-relief sex with Aaron. However, in between the amazing sex and a short power nap, I nailed down the unsub's personality and his possible next target, even with the lack of evidence on the case.

Passing through the metal detector and retrieving my property, I headed toward the elevators to the fifth floor, the location of my office. People crowded into the small metal box, mostly ignoring one another, checking their cell phones and watches. I gripped my purse and messenger bag in front of me and took a deep breath before my fear of tight spaces took over. At first, Rey used to laugh at my claustrophobia until he saw the crippling effect it had on me. I'd been dealing with it since college.

I focused on the numbers of each floor as they lit up, saying each one under my breath to distract myself from the tight confines of the elevator. If I hadn't been short on time, I would've taken the stairs like usual.

The car shuddered and jerked as it slowed to a stop. I exhaled a breath when the shiny metal doors slid open.

I exited the elevator, headed to my office. "Hey, Mr. Douglas, how are you doing this morning?" I asked the janitor when I exited the elevator on the way to my office.

He looked up from his mop and bucket. "I'm doing good, Dr. LaCroix. Make sure you have a safe and wonderful weekend."

"Will do." I waved. "And you do the same, Mr. Douglas."

I reached the sanctity of my office and placed my purse in my bottom desk drawer while Renee, my assistant, rattled off my schedule and messages. Thank goodness it was a short day. I had more packing to do before I headed home to see my grandparents. I only had a couple of things to wrap up in the office after the briefing with Mr. Steele, then I could get on with my much-needed extended vacation.

After gathering my messenger bag filled with the case files and my notes, I headed toward Mr. Steele's office to brief him, Renee still at my side.

"Renee, please take messages for all my calls, and let everyone know I'll be sure to return them before I leave for vacation since no one will be able to reach me. Thank you."

"No problem, Dr. LaCroix," she said, breaking off and heading in the opposite direction of Mr. Steele's office.

Walking down the long corridor the agents dubbed the "Hall of Fame." Plaques lined the walls, all commemorating federal agents' accomplishments going all the way back to the establishment of the Atlanta FBI field office. I thought about everything I had gone through to get to where I was today, including the loss of the one man I believed would be by my side through all this.

While I had applied for a position in the Louisiana field office, I'd been offered the position in Atlanta instead. It had been a difficult decision to make, but this was where I was needed. No matter if it were in Atlanta or Louisiana, I was determined to give a voice to those who could no longer speak, and my abilities were best served here, despite the cost.

It could be intimidating briefing Mr. Steele, but I was always confident in my abilities to give agents the best information possible to catch whoever they were looking for. In this case, the suspect was a child murderer, although the team didn't know that yet. While the agents believed Whitney Harry was the kidnapper's only victim, from my assessment, I believed there were more.

"Dr. LaCroix, it's nice to see you again," Stacy, Mr. Steele's secretary, said when I reached her desk.

"You too, Stacy. I have a briefing with Mr. Steele this morning."

She nodded. "Yes, ma'am. He and the others are waiting in the conference room."

Others?

From my understanding, this was supposed to be a briefing with only him, but he must've wanted the entire team updated due to my vacation and with it being a high-profile case. When I reached the conference room, I entered without knocking. Of course, when I crossed the threshold, all heads turned in my direction, and all the chatter ceased.

This was the usual reaction from men whenever I entered a room, especially when I was the only woman present. It was something I had to get used to. It was a man's world, and they didn't view women in the best light, especially a woman who could walk circles around them when it came to the job.

I made my way to the front of the room, my heels clicking against the tile floor. Each man rose from their seat as I passed. Some looked on with respect, others with lust, some with disgust. The judgmental glares and lust-filled stares came along with the job, but I ignored them the best I could. I focused on the respect I had gained not only within the Bureau but also outside of it.

I met the Agent-in-Charge at the head of the conference table and shook his outstretched hand. "Mr. Steele."

"Dr. LaCroix, it's nice to see you again. I hope you don't mind. I thought it best to brief the entire team since you'll be out of town for a while."

"Not a problem, sir. Are you ready to get started?"

He nodded, pulled out the seat next to him, and I sat while the men returned to their seats.

"Gentlemen, as you know, Atlanta PD has requested our help on this important case. Not that all cases aren't important, but the missing child is the granddaughter of Senator Thom Owens. So, you do realize there are special circumstances in this case. Everyone hopes we can find the child before the kidnapper does the unthinkable. That's why I've asked Dr. LaCroix to give us some insight into this kidnapper. Dr. LaCroix, you have the floor."

"Thank you, sir." I rose from my chair and removed my files and notes on the case from my bag, then turned my attention to the eight men seated on either side of the long conference room table. "Gentlemen, your kidnapper is more than likely a white male in his late twenties to early thirties. This man is not a novice. He's too organized for this to be his first kidnapping, and although the child has been missing for less than forty-eight hours, she is more than likely not alive."

Chatter and grumbles filled the room. I ignored the responses to my assessment. Although it was sad a child was missing, one I feared was dead, I couldn't let emotion play into my assessment. I always hoped for the best in all cases, especially those involving children. In this instance, the best-case scenario would be to find the child alive, but I always prepared for the worst. In this case, the worst was the most likely outcome.

"None of us want this to be the outcome, gentlemen, but with kid-nappings of children in this age range, by kidnappers of this particular demographic, they rarely keep their victims alive after the first few hours."

"And why is that, Dr. LaCroix?" Mr. Steele asked, his hands steepled and his leg crossed at the knee.

"Well, sir, a number of factors could play into a kidnapper's decision to kill the victim, including the gender of the unsub, the initial reason for the kidnapping, or whether he just feels like he wants to do it today or the next. In this case, the perpetrator is a younger male who took a young child.

Her death will be deliberate and, more than likely, due to asphyxiation. He wouldn't be able to pass up the chance to exert control over her."

"And why do you think he's White?" one agent asked, disdain marring his face. "There's nothing on the scene indicating the race of the suspect."

The older White man, in his mid-to-late fifties, looked at me like I couldn't dare tell him something he couldn't figure out for himself with his many years in law enforcement. His reaction almost caused me to roll my eyes.

Men.

This was the typical reaction working at a male-dominated agency. Men were intimidated by a strong, educated Black woman, especially in the law enforcement field. My ability to accurately profile a suspect was always questioned, despite my accuracy rate since I'd joined the agency and became one of the most accomplished behavioral analysts in the country. No matter how well I did my job, none of it mattered to most of these men.

"Agent?"

"Hoffman," he responded snidely as if I should already know his name.

Ignoring his tone and readying myself to show this ignorant ass how good I was at my job, I squared my shoulders and made sure to look him directly in the eye. This was another thing I'd learned while working with these agents over these past three years. They assumed because I was a woman, they could intimidate or bully me. My mother taught me that when you make assumptions about someone or something, you make an ass of yourself, like this agent was doing now. My father's words always infiltrated my thoughts when I was in situations like this—*you are a strong, intelligent Black woman. Do not ever let anyone think they are above you. Look them in the eye and show them why you are who you are, and why you are here.*

"Agent Hoffman, what do you remember about the crime scene?" I moved from behind the table, my arms crossed in front of me and my head tilted, never breaking eye contact with him while I waited for his response.

"It was in a suburban, upper-middle-class neighborhood." He tapped his pen against the legal pad in front of him. "Although not gated, it's virtually a no crime area other than teenage pranks. What does that have to do with the race of our suspect?"

"I will tell you what it has to do with your suspect, Agent Hoffman. It's not just a suburban, upper-middle-class neighborhood. A *White* suburban upper-middle-class neighborhood is how I would categorize the community. From my understanding, not one minority family lives in the subdivision. Do you agree?"

He nodded, and so did every other agent in the room.

I passed copies of my profile out to each agent in the room, including Agent Hart, who accepted with his panty-dropping smile. "And this is the main reason your unsub is most likely White. And do you know why that is, Agent Hoffman?"

I was being petty, but some people needed to be put in their places. Agent Hoffman was one of those people.

"No, I do not, Dr. LaCroix," he said, his voice sounding irritated. "But I'm sure you're going to tell me."

No need to get mad now because I'm showing you why I'm the best at what I do.

I smiled. "There's no way a person of color could walk through an all-White neighborhood, especially a *wealthy* all-White neighborhood, take a young, blond haired, blue-eyed White female from her front yard in broad daylight without neighbors noticing." Before he could protest with whatever asinine statement he wanted to make to discount my analysis, I continued. "Now, you are more than welcome to test my theory, but as a person of color, I can assure you, Agent Hoffman, that although I work for the FBI, even *I* couldn't walk through that neighborhood dressed in the attire I'm wearing today without garnering attention from neighbors. A person of color would stand out and be easily recognizable, especially a young Black male. So, your suspect is a well-dressed White male with an equally nice automobile because he could blend in with the neighborhood from his race, what he's wearing, and his vehicle. He's your typical 'boy next door' killer. Also, he probably used something to lure the young girl to his car. Puppy, candy, ice cream, doll, anything that would entice a child to speak to a stranger."

"How did you determine the gender of the killer?" Agent Johnathan Grant asked. "Couldn't a female with that same description also go unnoticed and entice a child with those same things?"

I had worked with Agent Grant on a couple of cases during my first year in Atlanta, and he was a stickler for details. So, it wasn't a surprise I had not gone through this briefing without him asking questions. It also wasn't a surprise Mr. Steele had placed him on this case. He was good, if not the best, at his job.

"Agent Grant, it's nice to see you again," I said, and he nodded. "As detailed in my profile of female kidnappers, they tend to lean more toward younger children than Whitney Harry. And those who do kidnap and eventually kill their victims, more often than not, the victims are their own children. Think along the lines of Susan Smith, who drowned her kids in her vehicle, or Andrea Yates, who drowned her kids in the bathtub. In this case, female family members have been cleared. Also, when there is a sexual component involved in a kidnapping of a child, around five percent are women, and there's some sort of emotional component to it."

"But are there exceptions to the rule?"

"Yes, Agent Grant, there are always exceptions to any rule, but my analysis is based on the evidence given to me." This was the part that everyone didn't understand about my job. I based my analysis on evidence, nothing more. "Remember, gentlemen, I'm not a psychic. I'm not a mind reader. My profiles are strictly based on the evidence provided to me, what the possibilities are based on case studies, and my experience in the field. And by the police reports, witness statements, and other evidence collected by the local police officers from the scene, as well as psychological studies of similar cases, your person of interest is a white male, not a white female."

"So, what is your conclusion, Dr. LaCroix?" Mr. Steele asked.

"My conclusion, based on the evidence provided to me, is Whitney Harry, age six, will be found discarded carelessly among having other traumas, including sexual assault. These are all signs that point to a male suspect who is of the same upper-middle-class upbringing but an outcast among his peers."

"Why would he kidnap someone so young?" Aaron asked.

"Typically, with female victims, no matter the age, it's sexual and about control."

"What else should we know?" Agent Grant asked.

"I believe your victim is not his first. I would search for other missing children of similar backgrounds as Whitney Harry and for victims of unsolved cases across the nation that fit her background. There is a reason your guy is targeting children like her."

"So, you don't think it has anything to do with Senator Owens like the locals are suggesting?" Aaron asked.

I shook my head. "Unless the Senator and his family are hiding something, no, I don't believe so. No ransom was demanded, and no political statements have been issued since her kidnapping. I actually think this may have been the first mistake he's made."

"How so?" Mr. Steele asked, sitting forward in his chair, eager to hear my thoughts.

"In the selection of his victims, he would be very meticulous, but in this case, his target was from a well-known political family in Atlanta, which garnered more attention than he may have intended," I said. "Which may point to him not being from the area, or he's only been living here for a short period of time. Also, gentlemen, I believe this man is a serial killer, and if that is the case, all serial killers have a signature, as well as a trigger. If you can identify his signature, which will link all his kills together, you will find your man and what triggered him to kidnap Whitney Harry and vice versa. Find the trigger, and you will find the signature."

"Thank you, Dr. LaCroix."

"You're welcome, Mr. Steele. Okay, gentlemen," I said, gathering the rest of my files. "If there are no more questions for me, I will be leaving so you can get to it. If questions arise, my contact information is included in your packet. Although I won't be able to be reached by phone for the next few weeks, please send me an email, and I'll respond in less than twenty-four hours if you have any questions. Also, Jerry Davidson will have the case file and my notes. He'll be able to help you as well if it's something urgent."

Mr. Steele stood and shook my hand. Then, I exited the conference room. This was a very tricky case, and the FBI would have to walk a tightrope trying to identify this killer due to the high-profile victim. If my analysis was correct, they had less than a month before another child went missing from this area or somewhere else in the country.

"Dr. LaCroix, you have a visitor," Renee said when I entered my office and sat at my desk. I looked at the clock on the wall and then sifted through the sticky notes stuck on my desk with the messages I needed to return before heading out of town.

"Who is it?" I asked, continuing to look through emails and other messages without looking up.

"A Detective LaCroix."

I stopped doing what I was doing but didn't look up at Renee, afraid of what my face might give away.

"I told him you were in a meeting and asked if he would like to leave you a message. He declined and said it was an urgent matter and that he needed to speak with you as soon as you were out of your meeting."

Numerous thoughts raced through my head. Was it Mama LaCroix? Even though I talked to her a few days ago, she hadn't been in the best health these past years after Mr. LaCroix passed from cancer. Could it be my family? Like me, Rey stayed in contact with my grandparents, who'd raised me, and they still considered him their grandson despite the divorce.

"Dr. LaCroix? What would you like me to tell him?" Renee asked, bringing me back from my wandering thoughts.

"I'm sorry, Renee. Tell the front desk to get him checked in, then send him up. You can escort him in. Thank you."

She nodded and left.

I stood and gazed out the floor-to-ceiling windows lining the back wall of my office, which gave a spectacular view of the Atlanta skyline. It was even more beautiful at night. Although my office was on the smaller side compared to some of the others on this floor, it had the best view by far. Looking out the window, I tried to tamp down my anxiety and excitement to see Rey again.

After three years, what did he want?

After waiting only a few minutes, I knew the exact moment he stepped into my office. The air in the room shifted like it always did when he was around.

"Thank you, Renee," I said without facing the man who still held my heart captive for all these years. "Please close the door, and make sure no one disturbs us."

"Okay, Dr. LaCroix."

The sound of the door shutting caused me to flinch slightly. I wrapped my arms around myself. We both stood in silence. I was sure he didn't know what to say because it was hard for me to talk as well.

"You look good, DeeDee," he said with a slight tremble in his voice.

I inhaled sharply, and my head dropped. His voice, deep and sensual, shocked my system. I knew I missed him. Certain smells, foods, and places always made me think of him, but up to that moment, I didn't realize how much until he spoke. The last time I heard his voice was the night I walked away from him. And, to keep myself from giving in to my desire to be with him and throwing away the opportunity to pursue my dream, I requested we have no contact throughout our divorce proceedings.

Three years was a long time not to hear from or see the one person you loved more than anything.

Tears slowly found their way down my cheeks, and I furiously wiped them away, taking a deep breath to compose myself.

Keep it formal, DeeDee. Don't let him see how much he still affects you.

"Detective LaCroix, how may I help you?"

I settled behind my desk, looking at the file folders laying on my desk instead of looking at him. I knew I would get lost in those beautiful eyes like I always did.

"DeeDee, look at me," he commanded.

I ignored him. I needed time to think and strengthen the wall around my heart I'd built when it came to him. I motioned to the chair sitting in front of my desk.

"Have a seat."

When I finally had the strength to face the man I'd longed to see over these past years, I looked at him. He was as handsome as I remembered, with stormy dark eyes staring back at me, shoulder-length jet-black hair pulled into a man bun I always enjoyed running my fingers through after a night of unadulterated sex, and his face covered in a full beard.

I leaned back in my chair and took in the man who held my heart while he did the same. The connection we shared was still there. The room was charged with it.

"Why are you here, Rey?" I pushed down the urge to run into his arms and finally feel those soft pink lips against mine again. "It's been three years."

I asked the question with a little more attitude than needed, but I had to hide how much he still affected me. Rey could read people like a book, and he was always in detective mode.

"I just couldn't bring myself to see you or hear your voice after you left," he said. "It was fucking hard, you know? It's still hard, and I didn't want to disrupt your life."

I nodded instead of responding. I understood what he meant. I knew if I saw him or heard his voice, I would drop everything and go back to him. That wasn't the best for me. This job was.

"But I had to push that aside because I need your help."

"You have a case?"

"Not just any case." He sighed. "I have a serial killer."

"In the parish?" I asked, surprised the small parish would have a serial killer. "Why haven't I seen anything on the news, or why hasn't it come across the FBI wire?"

"Yes, we have a serial killer in the parish, and the higher-ups are keeping a lid on it. Right now, the murders are only being reported on locally. With the number of bodies this guy is racking up, it won't be long before it becomes a national story."

"Rey, you know you have to go through official channels in order for the FBI to get involved, and your case definitely isn't coming across my desk here in Atlanta. But if you would like my help specifically, you could request the Louisiana field office call me in once the locals ask for their help."

"I know all that, DeeDee, but that's why I asked for *your* help, not the FBI's."

"Rey, this isn't like when I was in school, my job…"

He held up his hand, stopping my protest of getting involved in local matters without clearance from the FBI. I worked on cases both locally and nationally, but never without a request from the local authorities. Even with outside cases, prosecutors or defense attorneys that needed my help had to be cleared by Steele, and there was some sort of pissing contest the local and federal authorities had with one another. One I had been thrust in the middle of many times.

"Listen, Mama Wright told me you were heading home for an extended vacation."

"Of course, she did," I mumbled, rubbing my temples. "Why is my grandmother giving you details on what I'm doing, Rey?"

He smirked. "Because she loves me."

I shook my head, chuckling. He was right. My grandmother thought the sun rose and set on whatever Rey LaCroix did, and if this case got us to spend more time together, she would be all for it. She gave me hell for walking out on Rey like I did, although she understood why I had no other choice.

"Okay, give me the basics of the case, and I'll call you in a couple of days to see if I can make any headway."

I rose from my seat, walked around my desk, and stood in front of the man who still held my heart in his hands.

"Thank you. We need all the help we can get on this one. *I* need all the help I can get. It was good seeing you again, DeeDee." Gathering me into his arms, he held me tightly, his embrace feeling like home. "I missed you so much."

"It was good seeing you too, Rey."

I laid my head against his chest, inhaling his scent, listening to the sound of his heartbeat and relishing the feel of being in his arms again. I missed him too, but I kept that to myself. He tightened his hold as though if he let me go, I'd disappear. The tap on the door brought me out of the place I had longed to be for the past three years.

"Dana..." Aaron called out in a harsh tone, and I stepped out of Rey's arms.

"I'm sorry, Dr. LaCroix. I explained to Agent Hart you couldn't be disturbed, but he refused to listen," Renee angrily said.

"It's all right, Renee. I'll be with you in one minute, Agent Hart." I looked past Rey into the eyes of a man who looked like he wanted to burn the world to the ground.

Rey handed me the expandable file folder and had that smug ass smirk stretched across his face. He was up to something.

"Don't do it," I mouthed, causing his smile to widen.

Shit!

"It was good seeing you again, DeeDee, but no need to call me later. Mama invited me for the weekend." He looked down at the wristwatch I'd given him on our second wedding anniversary, then back at me. *Is he still wearing his wedding ring?* "My plane leaves in a couple of hours. I'll see you at home."

He leaned down, placing a kiss on my cheek.

"Did you have to say that?" I whispered in his ear where no one else could hear.

He stood, winked, and shrugged. He knew exactly what the hell he'd done. So, he knew who Aaron was. *Asshole.* He sauntered out of my office, bypassing Aaron, giving him his signature smirk.

Aaron was seething, and although we were in that off-again stage of our relationship, he'd made it clear what he wanted from me and had just been in my bed this morning. So, he had a right to be angry.

Before he could speak, I held up my hand, stopping him. It was time for me to be an adult and let Aaron go. He was too good of a man for me to string along. Comfort, sex, and the need for companionship caused me to cling to him, but I needed to be honest with him and with myself. I hadn't gotten over Rey, and I didn't know if I could, especially if he wanted me to help him with this case.

We would be around each other a lot more, and old feelings hadn't died. Well, at least on my end, they hadn't. Apparently, not on Rey's, either, since he still wore his wedding ring. Aaron deserved to know where I stood with him. I wasn't going to be his wife, and until I got over Rey, I couldn't be with him or anyone else.

"Shut the door, Agent Hart." I sat behind my desk. "We need to talk."

This conversation had been a long time coming.

CHAPTER FOUR

DETECTIVE REY LACROIX

NORTH CAROLINA

Arriving at the hotel in North Carolina, all kinds of thoughts swirled in my head. While I went to Dana for help on this case, it would be stupid to disregard my feelings for her. It was natural holding her in my arms, like I was home. From her scent to the feel of her body against mine, I missed everything about her. After this case was done, there was no way I'd walk away from her again. No matter what those damn papers said, Dana LaCroix was still my wife, and I was going to fix what I fucked up.

Recognition and jealousy hit me when Agent Hart stepped into Dana's office, breaking up our reunion. He'd appeared in photographs at events and nights out with her friends and colleagues, but just as much as I was jealous of him, he was also jealous of me. I took great pleasure in knowing that and looked at it as a good sign. It meant he knew about me because I still held a place in her heart. Hopefully, that place was large enough that he couldn't penetrate it. No matter how selfish it might sound, I wanted Dana happy, but not with another man because that meant what we had was over for good. I wasn't ready for it to be done.

I'd kept up with Dana's life after we split, and Agent Hart always got under my skin because it should have been me with her. I aimed to make sure she remembered the place I held in her life and her heart. Now, the only thing left to do was to convince my ex-wife that we belonged together and to give me a second chance. I'd do whatever it took to have her back in my life. I could never let Dana go completely; she was the love of my life.

Taking the elevator to the top floor of the hotel, I took out my phone from my pocket and dialed Lucile Wright. Although divorced from Dana, I remained close with her grandparents. I talked to both her grandmother and grandfather, Byron, at least twice a week to make sure they were doing all right and didn't need anything. Both were getting up in age and didn't have anyone around to make sure they had everything they needed. I wasn't able to visit as often as I'd liked since the divorce, but whenever I traveled to Charlotte for conferences or had some free time, I made sure to visit. I loved them like they were my own family.

"Son, DeeDee arrived about an hour ago," Mama Wright said as soon as she answered the call. "I'm serving supper in an hour. Make sure you're here *on time*, Rey."

I chuckled. Mrs. Wright was a drill sergeant when it came to being on time for breakfast, lunch, and dinner. If you were a minute late, you didn't get to eat at her table unless a natural disaster or something close to it kept you from being there when she wanted you to be there.

"Yes, ma'am. I will be there within the hour. Love you."

"I love you too, son," she said, ending the call.

After quickly jumping in and out of the shower to wash away the grime of multiple plane rides—first from Louisiana to Atlanta, then from Atlanta to North Carolina—I quickly dressed. The humidity in North Carolina was just as brutal as in Louisiana, so I decided to go simple and comfortable, dressing in a gray t-shirt and dark blue jeans for dinner. I grabbed the keys to my rental truck, cell phone, and room key, then headed out.

In less than thirty minutes, I arrived at the Wrights' rural home. This was one place I loved to visit outside of Louisiana. I was a country boy who loved to fish, hunt, and trap, and the damp rural air, heat, and bugs of North Carolina reminded me so much of home. The Wrights' home sat deep in a wooded area about a mile off a rural two-lane road in the middle of nowhere. It was a beautiful place, but it also worried me since the Wrights were older and didn't have a neighbor closer than a mile away.

Exiting the truck, I focused on the love of my life while she sat laughing with her grandfather in the white rocking chairs on the covered porch of the Wrights' home. I spent many days and nights sitting on this porch with DeeDee's family, some of those days with her over the course of our seven-year relationship and some without her after we divorced.

"Are you gonna just stand there gawking at my granddaughter all day long, boy?" Mr. Wright laughed. "Or are ya gonna come give an old man a hug?"

I slowly made my way onto the covered porch with a smile. "Can't I do both, old man?"

He scoffed, slowly stood, and embraced me, giving me a couple of slaps on the back before he sat back down into the rocking chair with a grunt.

"It's good to see ya, Pops. How ya been?"

"Can't complain, boy. Cannot complain. The fish are biting, and my woman is keeping me fed." He rubbed his rounded stomach, which had slimmed over the last year since illness had taken over. "No better life than this." He nodded, rocking back and forth in his rocking chair.

That was his response every time I asked the question whenever I visited or spoke to him on the phone. It had been a few months since I'd last come to see them, but I was glad I was here with them now. Pops had been having a tough time these past few months because of some health issues. So, it was good to see him outside for a change, breathing in the fresh air.

My attention then turned to my beautiful ex-wife. Her hair was pulled up in a loose ponytail high on her head. Her make-up-free skin glistened with a light sheen of sweat that my tongue itched to lick from her beautiful body. A beautiful purple strapless cotton dress clung to her curves when she stood to embrace me.

"Hey, Rey."

"Hey, DeeDee." I hugged her a little bit longer than I probably should have since she seemed to have a man in her life, albeit not for long if I had anything to say about it. "You look beautiful as always."

"Thanks," she mumbled.

"You gonna let her go, boy?" Pops chuckled as he stood and made his way to the front door.

I took a step back and rubbed the back of my neck.

"Make sure y'all don't get lost before dinner is served."

He made his way inside the house, shaking his head and mumbling about not wanting to hear his wife's mouth if we weren't on time for dinner.

We both started laughing.

Every time I spoke to Pops, he always made sure to tell me how much of an asshole I was for breaking Dana's heart, and I always agreed. However, I assured him I would do everything in my power to get her back, if she'd have me. Hopefully, with her helping me with my case, she'd give me the opportunity to rectify my mistake. Dana LaCroix was the love of my life, and I wanted her back.

I needed her back.

She returned to her rocking chair, and I took the one Pops had been sitting in, right beside her. We sat for a few moments, listening to the nature around us while she fanned herself with a church fan—the one with the picture of praying hands on the front.

"You want a fan?" She laughed as I wiped away the sweat beading up on my forehead with a handkerchief. "It's hot as hell out here."

"Nah, I'm good." I leaned forward with my forearms planted on my thighs. "It's hot, but not Louisiana hot."

"That is true."

"How ya been, DeeDee?" I looked over at her, and her eyes narrowed. "And I'm not talking about the job. I know how that's going. I want to know how you've been?"

"Why do you care, Rey?" she snapped, her expression clouded in anger. "You let me leave, remember? How I'm doing isn't your concern anymore."

I deserved every curse and every glare she aimed at me. I was the one who let her walk away. To be honest, I thought she wouldn't, and if she did, she wouldn't file for divorce. My arrogance cost me a lot, so I deserved everything she threw my way.

But she was wrong. When I vowed through the good times and bad, until death did us part, I meant every fucking word. I still wore my wedding ring, although we weren't together anymore, because Dana LaCroix would always be my concern. She would always be my wife.

"Be angry all you want, DeeDee. I deserve it. I asked for everything you can throw at me because I didn't fight for us, but you'll always be my concern, whether we're together or not."

Silence engulfed us while she searched nervously for the meaning behind my words.

I leaned back in the rocking chair.

"Does Chanel know you're here with me?" she retorted in cold sarcasm, breaking our silence after a few minutes.

My brows drew together, and I glared at her. What the hell did Chanel have to do with anything my wife and I discussed? I never understood why

DeeDee was so hung up on her. Chanel and I fucked each other before I met her and again now that we were divorced. There was nothing special about Chanel Boudreaux, but DeeDee always had an issue with her.

"Why in the hell would Chanel know anything about what I'm doing?"

There was a little more anger in my tone than there should have been, but I didn't want to talk about Chanel. I wanted to talk about DeeDee, about us.

"Never mind," she mumbled, standing up. "It's none of my business."

When she tried to walk past me, I stood and grabbed her by the arm. She stopped and looked up at me with those large, round, doe eyes I missed so much.

"Anything that goes on in my life is your concern, DeeDee. No matter what those fucking papers we signed say or who we're fucking at the time. I'm your husband, and you're my wife. Always."

She took a sharp breath and stared, tongue-tied, until Mama Wright broke our trance by calling us inside for dinner.

"Dr. LaCroix, I'm gonna get you back. So, prepare yourself, my beautiful wife. I'm coming for you."

I motioned for her to go inside ahead of me.

Her eyebrows shot up in surprise, and she adamantly shook her head. "You can't be serious, Rey! You're fucking crazy if you think me helping you with this case changes anything between us. You let me go, remember? That was your choice, not mine. We've both moved on."

"I do remember, and it was the biggest fucking mistake of my life. But this right here, us together now," I caressed her face, "changes everything, my love. Every. Fucking. Thing."

I placed my hand on the small of her back, giving her a slight push so we could walk inside her grandparents' home.

I'd made my intentions known. Fuck Aaron Hart. If she thought I gave a damn about their relationship, she had another thing coming. Dana LaCroix was my wife. The love of my life. I'd made a mistake by not fighting for us, and it wasn't a mistake I'd make again.

I'd gotten a second chance to show her we belonged together.

We were meant to be.

* * * * * * * * * *

"That was amazing, Mama Wright." I rubbed my stomach. "I haven't had a homecooked meal like that in a while."

One of the reasons I loved coming here was eating whatever Mama Wright cooked. My mother was a great cook. Her Cajun food was out of this world, and since she'd been sick, she didn't cook much anymore. However, Mama Wright's food was on a different level, and she fed me until I was bursting at the seams.

"You're very welcome, baby." She beamed at the compliment. "I know you came to get baby girl's help on something, so I wanted y'all to be able to work on full stomachs."

"Thanks, Grandma. We're going to take over the den if that's all right with you?"

"Sure, baby. And Rey, you take the spare bedroom when you're done. I don't want you traveling late at night when y'all get finished," she said, continuing to clear the dishes off the table. "Since y'all ain't married no more, ya can't be doing no shacking up in this house."

"Grandma!"

"What, girl? Don't Grandma me. Y'all must think I'm a fool or something," Mama Wright mumbled. "I know what I see. When y'all start acting right again and get remarried, then y'all can share a room."

"Grandma, Rey and I are just working on a case, that's all. We are not getting back together."

"Whatever you want to think, DeeDee," Pops interjected, chuckling and pointing at me. "That boy has that same look he had the very first time I met him."

I leaned back in my chair and listened. Both her grandparents were right. My intentions were to get my wife back, and there was no need to hide it from the most important people in her life and mine.

"Tell them, Rey."

"Tell them what exactly, DeeDee?" I looked directly at my ex-wife and winked. "I messed up. I'm gonna fix it."

She stood and glared. "What is the matter with you?"

She threw her hands up in the air and stomped out of the room. She was furious, but I needed to let her grandparents know I was going to fight for her.

Her grandfather chuckled.

"Make it right, Rey," her grandmother said.

"I'm gonna try my best, Mama." I kissed her on the cheek, then followed Dana into the den.

"Did you have to say that, Rey?" she asked as soon as I walked into the room.

"Say what, Dana?" I shrugged like it was no big deal because, to me, it wasn't. I knew I'd fucked up. I'd known it was a mistake as soon as I signed my name on the divorce papers. "That I'm gonna fix what I messed up?"

"Yes, that!" She tossed her hands into the air, then started pacing. "You know how they feel about you, about us being together. You can't go filling their heads with the hope that we'll get back together when that's not going to happen."

"I do know how they feel, and that's why I told them the truth." I sat on the couch, pulled the files I'd handed her earlier from her messenger bag, and placed them on the table. "I told you, DeeDee, what my plans were. Did you think I was lying? You know me better than that."

"Rey, you can't be serious." She stopped pacing and glared at me with her hands on her hips. "We haven't been together for three years. I haven't heard from you in three fucking years!"

"That doesn't mean shit to me, DeeDee. None of it! I still love you, and I will love you until I take my last fucking breath. And you still love me, too. I know you do. You don't have to say it now, but I know you." I ignored her shocked look. We'd come back to this topic later. Right now, this case needed to be solved before he killed someone else. "Now, could you please sit your beautiful ass down and help me catch this son of a bitch?"

She remained standing for a few more minutes before she sighed and sat down beside me. "This conversation is not over," she mumbled.

"I know. So, did you get a chance to look at any of this?" I asked, glad she was ready to get started.

She nodded and picked up a sheet of paper from the file. "I did."

"Okay, so what did you get?"

"Without having time to dig deep into this, I could only come up with a preliminary workup."

"That's fine." And just like that, it was like old times. We were a team again. I flipped through the papers and photographs. "Something is better than nothing because we ain't got shit on this psycho."

"Okay, with your victims being college-educated women with high-pay-ing jobs averaging anywhere from two-hundred and fifty to five hundred thousand a year, more than likely, so does your unsub. These women all have white-collar jobs and make an incredibly good living. They also lived in affluent neighborhoods. I would say your killer is of a similar background. He's highly educated, probably a White male who went through a recent life-changing event such as a divorce or loss of a job. That's more than likely when the killings started."

"Why do you think he's highly educated?"

"Women usually tend to have something in common with the men they date. For example, we both have an interest in criminology, me the behavioral and psychological side, and you the enforcement side. Women who are executives, such as these women, tend to gravitate to men of similar education, of similar backgrounds—wealth, friends of the same social circle, expensive cars. These women aren't picking up random men from bars."

"And race? Why not an African American man or another man of color? There are plenty of men of every race who are affluent."

"I know, but I'm basing my assessment on the killer's use of rope. It is rare for men of color to use rope in this manner—not unheard of, but rare. Also, his wife or girlfriend would also be highly educated, probably African American as well."

"So that would be his trigger? Either a divorce or job loss?" I asked, making sure I left no stone unturned with this guy and making a note in my notebook. When Dana used to help with other cases, she would always say, "If we can identify the killer's trigger and signature, we can identify the killer."

"Yes, something along those lines. I would lean more toward a divorce, but it also could be both. A job loss that caused his divorce, maybe." She picked up a crime scene photo of two of the victims as they were being pulled out of the water. Then she picked up another picture of the same two women on the slab at the morgue. "These women are around the same age, and they all have similar features, all African American, so I think your killer is killing his wife, possible girlfriend, or someone he's obsessed with over and over again."

She tossed down that picture and picked up another. After a few minutes of scrutinizing the image of the bound women, she picked up another photo and put those two side by side.

I could sit back and watch Dana work all day. There were many times me and Amir brought our cases to her when we would get stuck. What would take us months to figure out would take her around a week or less.

She pulled all the photos from the file folder and laid them side by side across the coffee table, running her fingers over the photograph. "You see something?"

I picked up one of the pictures and looked at it from every angle before placing it back down.

"I don't see shit. Haven't seen shit for months."

Although she didn't answer, I knew she heard me, but she was laser-focused on something in the pictures. She ran her finger over the image of the ropes the women had been bound with.

"What type of rope was used?" she asked without looking up at me, continually running her fingers over the bindings.

"Jute."

"With every victim?"

I flipped through my notes to make sure I answered correctly before responding. "Yes. Every victim was bound with jute."

"Natural rope," she absently stated.

"Is that significant?"

She tilted her head and continued to stare at the rope bindings. "Yes. You see here?" She pointed to a specific section of the intricately tied rope, tracing her finger down the bindings.

I nodded. "Yeah. I know how he did it is important, but I don't know why it's important."

"I think this is Kinbaku. I'm not sure, though. We may need to consult an expert to make sure."

"Kinbaku?"

"Yes. It means 'tight binding' in Japanese. Was the length of the rope the same for each girl?"

She picked up two pictures and laid them side by side.

I flipped through my notebook again to make sure I gave her the correct information. "Yes. Each rope was somewhere between twenty-three and twenty-six feet."

"Okay. I really think this is Kinbaku. In the West, Kinbaku is usually done with multiple ropes between twenty-three and twenty-six feet. In the East, the rope lengths are much shorter. He's staying true to the art by using specific techniques and even natural rope, but why bind two girls together? What's the significance of the number two to this killer?"

I scratched my head. That was the same question I had been asking myself. Why bind the two victims together? And why in the hell was he using a Japanese binding technique?

"That's why I came to you, so you could answer some of these questions."

She threw her head back and laughed like she was sincerely amused. "Rey, some questions only the killer can answer. I can get into a killer's head only so much. One thing that ties every serial killer together, though, is they enjoy the power of having life and death in their hands. That's what makes them want to keep killing again. Remember, it's about control."

"Could that be the reason for the bindings? A way to show he has control?"

"It's very possible, but I would need more evidence to tie the bindings to that thought. Death by asphyxiation, right?"

"Yeah, strangulation. They all have ligature marks around their necks, possibly from the rope they were bound with."

"So, I would say the asphyxiation aspect of the murder is more about control than the bindings. The ability to control whether someone can breathe is the ultimate control. He can squeeze to cut off her breaths and release to make sure she gets air, so she doesn't die," she said, mimicking the actions with her hands. "The ability to control whether death comes or not. But, like I said, I would need more evidence to tie the bindings to this killer's possible motive."

"No evidence was found other than the bindings. No semen, finger-prints, and not so much as a strand of fucking hair. We do know that the victims did have sex, but there were no signs pointing to forced penetra-tion. We can't tie the sexual intercourse to the murderer."

"Well, we can speculate you have your possible trigger, which is a divorce, job loss, or both. And you definitely have your signature, which is the binding. He's more than likely into the BDSM scene and women who are into rope play. I don't know how prevalent the scene is down in the parish, but it's possible he found his victims online, or wherever these ladies disappeared from, there could be a club. If that's the case, it would be an exclusive site or club. Individuals with this type of money like to keep their kinks secret or separated from their everyday lives and families. Rope play is a part of the scene, but using Kinbaku...he's had some training in the art. It's obvious with how good his binding technique is. See here."

She pointed to how the ropes were tightly wrapped around one woman's wrist and how it then wrapped around her body in a complex pattern. "He's been trained by a rope master," she continued. "The bindings and patterns are too well done and very intricate for a beginner. He may be a rope master himself."

"How do you know so much about this shit?" I asked, genuinely interested in how she learned so much about BDSM. We'd had some wild nights. Nights where I'd tie her up and blindfold her before fucking the shit out of her, but never something as crazy as what she was explaining now. "I know we had our times, but nothing like this."

She stared at me, her cheeks turning a vivid crimson. "Actually, when I was in graduate school, I studied the psychological effects on prisoners of war who were restrained using *Hojōjutsu* for a class project, which is the foundation of Kinbaku. Since it was connected, we also researched BDSM and rope play. How participants gain pleasure from pain."

"I need you to come home with me and help with this," I blurted out.

She groaned and sat back in the couch. "Rey, this is my vacation. I've worked so many cases this year, I need a break."

"DeeDee, there's no way I can do this without you. This guy is smart. He's dumping the bodies in the same bayou, and the women aren't even from the area. They're all from different towns more than fifty miles away."

Her eyebrows shot up in surprise.

"What bayou?"

"Laurels."

"The one you used to take me to?"

"Yep. The one and only. I think that was the first place I took you fishing, right?"

"Yeah, it was. There's some significance to this area for him. It could range from him liking its seclusion or he took his wife fishing there, like you did me. Something along those lines. But to use the same dumping ground, he most definitely has a connection to Laurels Bayou. And since none of the victims are from there, why did he choose your parish?"

I shrugged. This was why I needed Dana to come home. These details that took her only an hour to share with me, Amir and I might have never uncovered. If she didn't agree to help us, we might never catch this guy, and more women and their families would suffer.

"This is what I'm talking about, DeeDee. I would have never thought of anything like the connection to the area or that Kinbaku shit." I reached for her hand, intertwining our fingers. She didn't pull away, and my heart soared in my chest. "I really need your help with this, sweetheart."

"You're laying it on thick, Detective LaCroix."

"Is it working?"

"Rey, *if* I do this, and that's a big if, we need to set some boundaries."

Boundaries? What the fuck does she mean, boundaries?

"I'm coming in as a personal favor to you," she continued.

"Okay," I agreed, nodding. "I'm cool with that."

"Which means, I will not use my FBI credentials for your case in any way since I haven't been formally brought in by your department. I am your personal consultant."

"I can agree to all that. So, you'll come?" I asked impatiently.

She held up her hand. "I'm not finished. I have one more stipulation."

"Okay. I'm sure it can be done."

"I'll be staying at a hotel, not your home."

I do not agree.

I shook my head.

"Rey." She sighed.

"Now, wait one damn minute, DeeDee. There's no reason for you to stay in a hotel when you can stay with me in *our* home. I'd be damned if I let *my* woman stay in some hotel when she should be with me."

Why in the hell did she think I would ever agree to something like that? She wasn't about to stay in some hotel when she could stay with me. Unless this was about Agent Hart.

"Your woman?" she shouted. "You've lost your damned mind. Do you hear how crazy you sound right now?"

"Yes! My woman. Is this about Agent Hart?" I asked, my tone laced with anger. "You scared he'll get pissed?"

"Rey, you have no right to ask me anything about anyone in my life." She snatched her hand from mine. "You gave up that right three years ago! Now, if you want my help, there's no way I'm staying with you. We're not married anymore, and I sure as hell don't want to see you and your girlfriend together in my house!"

So, now I got it. My beautiful ex-wife was just as jealous of Chanel as I was of Agent Hart, even though she didn't have a reason to be. There wasn't anything serious going on between Chanel and me. Our arrangement only consisted of drunk fucking, nothing more. It was nowhere near as serious as what was going on with Agent Hart.

I sat back in the couch and rested my hands behind my head as a wide grin stretched across my face, which only made her even angrier.

"Your house, huh?"

She tilted her head to the side and pursed her lips. "What are you talking about?"

"You said your house." My grin widened. "So, now I get it. You're jealous."

"Whatever, Rey. I am not jealous of whatever you have going on with *that* woman. If you want some bleach-blonde skank who looks like she hasn't eaten anything in years, then have at it. As I said, I'll stay at a hotel, and we can work either from my room or at Amir and Delaney's, but I *will not* step foot in that house ever again."

She stood and stomped upstairs to her room.

"Well, at least she didn't say no," I mumbled, then smiled.

I looked down at my watch, and with the late hour, I decided not to follow her. I could explain away whatever assumptions she had about me and Chanel tomorrow after my impromptu fishing trip with her grandfather. Knowing Pops, he'd be up before the crack of dawn.

With all the travel finally catching up with me, I yawned while picking up the photographs of the victims. While I hadn't been able to take my long weekend to wallow in my misery, I got the chance I'd longed for since she walked away. I got to spend time with the most wonderful woman in the world and make my way back into her heart.

Staring at the photos of each victim, an eerie feeling slowly crawled its way over my skin, finally settling in the pit of my stomach. It was a feeling I'd learned over the years not to ignore. I looked at it as the universe's way of letting me know something was coming. There was something crucial I was missing about this case.

"There's something familiar about these women," I mumbled, running my hand through my hair, "but what?"

I stared at the pictures a few minutes longer, hoping something would click, but it didn't.

I pushed the eeriness away. I'd figure it out later.

I picked up the files and placed them back in the file folder. There was no way I wanted to hear Mama Wright tear us a new one for leaving these photos splayed across her table. I'd promised these women's families I would find the person who'd done this to their children, and now with Dana on board, that would be done sooner rather than later.

Although time wasn't on my side, the playing field was now even. I was gonna catch this motherfucker. *We* were gonna catch him. Together.

Chapter Five

Dr. Dana LaCroix

Louisiana

Rey and I had only been back in Louisiana for two days, and it almost seemed like old times. *Almost.* Of course, he tried to convince me to stay with him at his home, and I still refused. Too many memories were embedded in walls, the floors. I knew everywhere I turned, both good and bad memories would assault me—from celebrating our closing on the house and our first night as husband and wife in our bedroom, to the night I walked away. Whether good or bad, I didn't want the memories I'd shared with Rey to be tainted by the realization Chanel Boudreaux had been in the home we decided to share and spend the rest of our lives in together.

Rey was right when he said I was jealous of his relationship with her. He swore there wasn't a relationship for me to be jealous of when he'd tried to explain the dynamics of whatever they had going on the day before we left my grandparents' home. Since then, we'd been so consumed with his case, we hadn't gotten into it again, but I was curious. Chanel painted quite a different picture than Rey.

Rey's no longer married to me, so why does it even matter? His relationships aren't my concern, like my former relationship with Aaron isn't his.

Chanel Boudreaux became a thorn in my side as soon as Rey ended their sexual relationship. Then, after I went to live with Rey and eventually married him, she would show up whenever I was alone in town. It was like she'd been lurking around the corner, waiting for me to be alone, so she could approach me. Rey thought I was overexaggerating, but I wasn't. She probably celebrated our divorce, and of course, he went back to her instead of fighting for us. That thought crushed me.

Maybe she means more to him than I realized.

"This isn't what you're here for, DeeDee." I tried to clear my mind of my sour thoughts. "Help Rey solve this case, get back to your vacation, and then back to Atlanta. Far, far away from Rey LaCroix."

Spreading the crime scene, autopsy, and random photos of the victims across the bed, I examined everything from the placement of the bodies on the water to the intricate binding technique the killer used. The answer to our questions had to be in the bindings. It was his signature.

I traced my fingers over the rope, then placed my finger against my lips and tilted my head. "What am I missing?"

One thought barely crossed my mind before another followed.

"What is the significance of binding them together? Of all things, why are you using Kinbaku?" I paced at the end of the bed. "Think, DeeDee, think. Why would a killer do this?"

The knock at the door stopped me in my tracks, pulling me from my thoughts. Glancing down at my watch and noting the late hour, I hadn't been expecting anyone. I'd heard from Rey and Amir earlier, both saying they weren't going to be able to go over the case tonight.

I ambled barefoot to the door and looked through the peephole. When Rey raised the bag of takeout in the air, I shook my head and pulled the door open. "What are you doing here? It's late."

"It is late, but I know you. You haven't eaten anything worth a damn today, have you? You gonna let me in?"

I stepped aside, allowing him to enter. He placed the bags of takeout on the small round table near the window of the hotel room. I closed the door, ignored the mouthwatering smells, and walked over to the bed, observing the pictures *again*. I was missing something. I just couldn't put my finger on it.

"You know me so well." I continued to stare at the pictures, my back to him, forgetting about the delicious food he'd brought.

What am I not seeing?

Rey was right. Usually, whenever I got lost in a case, I might not eat more than a banana and drink a bottle of water that day. Today, I'd had two bottles of water and fruit from the complimentary fruit basket the hotel had provided. The place wasn't five stars and had no room service, but the sheets were clean, the queen-sized bed was comfortable, and it was in a decent part of the parish. It would work until I finished helping with the case.

"I do know you, possibly better than I know myself. Now get your beautiful ass over here and eat before I call Mama and tell her you're not taking care of yourself."

"You wouldn't dare!"

We laughed.

I couldn't help the excitement bubbling in my system. It was good to be back in Louisiana, to be back with Rey. I missed the place, and I missed him even more.

"Is this what I think it is?" I asked when we both sat down at the small table by the window.

I sniffed the mouthwatering smells from my favorite food and barely controlled my gasp of surprise. He handed me a bottle of water.

"It is. Now eat."

When I first moved to Louisiana, Rey bought me my first po' boy, and it quickly became my favorite Louisiana dish. Even though I'd traveled back to the parish since moving to Atlanta, I hadn't had the chance to eat one, especially one from my favorite restaurant, *Milly's*.

I rubbed my hands together. "I haven't had one of these bad boys in three years."

I picked up the sandwich, took a huge bite, and groaned when the bursts of flavors hit my tongue. The shrimp, tomatoes, and the Cajun seasonings of the remoulade sauce did a happy dance on my tongue. My eyes fluttered in total bliss, and when I opened them, Rey was staring at me.

I ignored the look dancing in his eyes.

Although I would have loved nothing more than to drown myself in everything Rey LaCroix offered, he'd made it clear when we were married that he wouldn't leave his job for me, and nothing had changed.

I still loved Rey. Loved him with everything in me, but I also loved my job. Atlanta was my home now, and Louisiana was still his.

"There's something we're missing with these murders, Rey. I can't put my finger on it."

I hoped focusing on the case would erase that look from his eyes, so we wouldn't do something we both might regret. Every cell in my body craved Rey. Everything about him.

"I know." He wiped his mouth with his napkin. "My gut is telling me the same thing. There's a specific reason he's targeting these women, my parish, and it has nothing to do with it being the perfect place to dump a body. It goes deeper. This bastard is meticulous. Everything has a reason."

"I still believe he's killing his wife, girlfriend, or someone he's obsessed with. These women aren't random. He chose them for a specific reason. I believe it's more, too. But the question is, what?" I took another bite of my sandwich and took a swig of water. "What is the significance of your parish? He's targeting the parish and that specific bayou, but why?"

"Maybe he's got it out for someone in the parish?" he asked, shrugging.

"Very possible. If that's the case, it would be someone in authority. He's giving that person the middle finger by dumping bodies there. Like a 'catch me if you can' deal."

Rey nodded, but the ringing of his cell interrupted our conversation. He placed what was left of his sandwich down on the wrapper and grabbed his phone, which he'd clipped to the waistband of his khaki slacks. He looked at the caller id and rubbed his forehead.

"Yeah, Amir?"

By the scowl on his face, I knew this call couldn't be good. When we'd been together, the late-night phone calls had come way too often. That was the price of being married to a homicide detective—a lot of lonely nights. But I was proud of him. He was a great detective. One of the best in Louisiana.

Late-night phone calls weren't a good sign, and by the reports on the local news, the parish had been plagued with gun violence for months, along with these killings. I still couldn't believe the police had been able to keep all these women's deaths off the national news.

"All right, I'll see you in fifteen." Rey ended the call.

"Duty calls, huh?"

I was sad to see him go, but we both had work to do.

I took the final bite of my sandwich, stood, and tossed my trash into the bin sitting next the table.

"Always." He ran his fingers through his hair before placing it in a bun. "There's a turf war going on right now."

"Yeah, I've seen the news reports."

"The rival gangs have been going at each other for months. This will be the third gang-related homicide in two weeks."

"Damn."

Tiredness and stress covered his face. That was one thing about working in law enforcement, especially dealing with homicides. No matter what case you were working on, the job never stopped. His job never stopped. It didn't matter if there was a serial killer; he also had other cases that needed to be solved.

Rey stood, picking up his trash, tossed his unfinished food in the trash bin, and then walked toward the door.

"Thanks for bringing me dinner," I said when we reached the door. "It was so good."

He pushed the stray hair that had fallen from my messy bun behind my ear. "No problem. I'll always take care of you, DeeDee."

He leaned down and placed a kiss on my forehead before he opened the door and walked out into the hallway. "Make sure you lock the door."

"I will. Be safe out there, Rey."

He winked. "Always. I love you, DeeDee."

My body stiffened. This was the second time he told me he loved me, and it had me more confused than ever.

Rey still loves me. What the hell's going on?

Without waiting for a response, he walked down the hallway, not looking back. When he stepped into the elevator, I closed and locked the door, then engaged the security latch. With my back against the door, I tried to catch my breath. It finally hit me.

He was serious.

He wanted me back.

I pushed any thoughts of Rey and his confession to the back of my mind. I couldn't get lost in what was happening between us. The Black women of Louisiana were depending on me to find this bastard.

With a full stomach and the adrenaline flowing, it would be a late night and early morning for me. I might get two hours of sleep.

I strolled over to the end of the bed, and, once again, the photographs of the dead women ensnared me. There was something so familiar about these women.

But what?

After hours of going through photos and Rey's notes, nothing clicked. I glanced down at my watch. It was well past two o'clock in the morning, but I wasn't giving up. This guy was smart, but I was smarter.

"Black women, around the same height, professionals, with very similar features. What are you trying to tell me?" I picked up one of the photos. "You have an attraction to Black professional women, seemingly those who are into BDSM. Or maybe you're just into it and tie them up after you kidnap them. But if that's true, where are you meeting them?" I drew the photograph closer, staring. Dissecting every last little detail, from the position of the bindings to how tightly they were bound, leaving deep purple bruises on their dark skin.

Oh shit!

"What the hell is that?" I picked up a different picture, then another one to see if I saw it on the others. "Yes! It's on every photograph. How in the hell did I miss that?" I said to the empty room, excited I'd finally had a breakthrough. "All the bodies have it tied within the bindings. The infinity symbol."

I rubbed my forehead.

"A promise of eternal love? That could be why he's dumping them in twos. Binding them together in death for eternity."

My head shifted to the door at the sound of something being shoved under the bottom. I walked over and looked through the peephole. Nothing. I picked up the manilla envelope and opened it, pulling the paper out.

Welcome home, DeeDee. I missed you so much. I wish I could have followed you to Atlanta, but I was indisposed at that time, but she'll no longer be an issue.

Did you get the letters I sent you? Probably not. I know the FBI screens things, and I haven't been able to find out where you live yet, but now that you're here, that's no longer an issue. Looks like my plan worked. It took a while to get him to call you. That asshole detective isn't fit to breathe the same air as you, but I'll take care of him soon enough. I'm so excited you're finally back where you belong—with me.

I hope you liked your gifts. Although none of them were a good enough replacement for you, I had to make do with what I could until you returned. Eventually, I'll have the real thing, and we'll be bound together in death for eternity.

"Gifts?" My brows furrowed. "What the fu..."

The paper slipped from my hands, floating to the carpet. With trembling hands, I walked over to the table, grabbed my cell phone, and called the only person who could help.

"DeeDee, what's wrong, baby?" His voice sounded tired but concerned.

"Rey, the killer. He gave...I believe he left me a letter."

"Fuck! Okay, I'm on my way. Don't open the door unless it's me."

I nodded.

"DeeDee!"

"Rey." My voice trembled. I'd been this scared only one other time in my life. I didn't know what to think. I didn't know what to do.

"I know you're scared, honey. I'm on the way. I promise. Don't open the door unless it's me, okay?"

"Okay."

CHAPTER SIX

DETECTIVE REY LACROIX

It had to be a sick joke or misunderstanding. It just had to be. There was no fucking way my killer had contacted Dana. No way.

I drove like a bat out of hell to get to her, ignoring all traffic laws, totally disregarding my safety and others. It took me less than fifteen minutes to pull up in front of her hotel.

I quickly jumped out of my truck and ran through the front door of the hotel past the door attendant—who swiftly followed me, trying to get me to stop—as I rushed through the lobby. There weren't any customers milling about, probably because it was three in the morning. The desk attendant was the only one sitting in the reception area, engrossed in whatever she was looking at on her phone.

"Sir!" the doorman frantically yelled, catching the attention of the desk attendant. "You can't leave your vehicle parked there! Sir!"

I didn't have time to explain why I didn't give a fuck about what he had to say. My focus was getting to my wife.

"Sir, you're parked in a fire zone!"

"Police business," I responded without looking and flashed my badge, silencing the doorman's protests and sending the desk attendant back to her station.

The stairs were my only option. I'd take the risk of being ambushed in a stairwell, where I had a fighting chance, over being caged inside an elevator.

My heart raced. My emotions swirled. Rage, confusion, but most of all, fear covered me.

How does the killer know who she is? How does he know where she's staying?

Fear and rage knotted inside me. He obviously had eyes on her, which caused my anxiety to increase even more. I took the stairs two at a time until I made it to the third floor and pounded on Dana's hotel room door.

"Open the door, DeeDee! It's me!"

The door flung open, and she jumped into my arms. I tightened my arms around her trembling frame before I kissed the top of her head. "It's all right, baby. I'm here. I'm not going to let anything happen to you. Are you alright?"

"Yes," she mumbled against the crook of my neck. "A little frazzled, but I'm fine."

"Where's the letter?"

She removed herself from my arms and pointed to the floor in front of the bed, where a white piece of paper lay. The crime scene photos and files were in the same place, spread across the bed, which meant she hadn't slept.

"You haven't been asleep, have you?" I asked, trying to take her mind off what was happening, if possible. I yanked out a clear evidence bag and blue latex gloves from my back pocket, pulled the gloves on, then photographed the lined notebook paper. After taking the picture, I picked it up and read the messy cursive writing.

"You know how I get when there's a case," she muttered.

I did. She forgot to take care of herself. That was why I'd made sure to bring her something to eat. I should have forced her to come home with me. Being alone wasn't safe.

"How long after I left did you get this?"

"Right before I called you. It was pushed under the door. I was working, and I had a breakthrough on the case."

"So, you didn't see who dropped it off?"

"No. I looked through the peephole after I heard it come under the door, but no one was there. At least, no one I could see."

"You didn't open the door and look out?"

She shook her head.

Good!

"Why do you think this is from the killer?"

"Because of how he signed it. The infinity symbol."

My eyes shifted to the bottom of the letter, and sure enough, there was an infinity symbol instead of a signature.

"That's the breakthrough I had on the case. The infinity symbol is in the bindings on all the victims, and that may be why he is binding them together."

I sent a text to Amir about the note to get a search warrant so we could get the footage from the hotel and to meet me at my home by seven. The sun would be up, and that would give us enough time to get some sleep. After pressing send, I pushed the phone into my back pocket.

"Get your shit. You're coming home."

"Rey, I don't think that's necessary."

I must've been hearing things. Not necessary? A freaking psycho had dropped off a letter in the early morning hours saying he missed her and how they'd be together in death, and she didn't think coming home with me was necessary?

"You've got to be fucking kidding me, DeeDee." I placed the letter back into the envelope it came in, put the envelope in the evidence bag, and placed it on the bed. I stalked over to the closet, pulled her suitcase out for her, and started throwing her shit in it since she was still stuck in the same spot. "You've lost your goddamn mind if you think I'm leaving you here after what just happened."

"Rey, I'm not going with you."

"It wasn't a fucking request, Dana LaCroix." I stopped tossing her shit into her suitcase and looked at her. "Get the rest of your shit, so we can go. Now!"

She gave me a hostile glare, which I returned. Rarely did I ever raise my voice at her, but I wasn't budging on this. This wasn't about our relationship. It was about her fucking safety. Whether she lived or died.

"Look, you can be pissed at me all you want. I don't fucking care. You're not staying here! Get your shit, like I said."

A crazed killer had gotten too close to her. It pissed me off and scared me shitless, all at the same time. Even if I had to throw her over my fucking shoulder like a damn caveman or cuff her ass, she was coming home with me. I let her pull this bullshit about staying in this damn hotel when I knew she should have been in our home, safe, with me.

But what happens when she's not with you? He's coming for her, and she can't be with you twenty-four seven.

My thoughts taunted me. I couldn't be with her twenty-four hours a day, seven days a week, but damn it, I'd try. Her staying here wasn't an option. There was no security, no one to protect her if this maniac came back. I raked my hand through my hair and paced the floor, rage building inside me. I was pissed at myself. Pissed I hadn't made the connection sooner. How could I have put her in danger? I'd done exactly what he wanted and brought her back to Louisiana. I'd been the one to put her in danger.

"I knew there was something familiar about these women. I just couldn't put my damn finger on it. I've done exactly what that motherfucker wants."

"Rey, stop." Dana placed her palms on my chest to stop me from pacing. "Calm down. What are you talking about?"

I sat on the end of the bed with my face in my hands. "At your grandparents', when you went to bed after we discussed the case, I got that feeling when I looked at the photos of all those women. At their graduation pictures, family photos, and autopsy photos. It's the first time I've gotten it."

Her eyes shot up in surprise. "*Your* feeling?"

I nodded. She knew exactly what I was talking about. When we were together, I had discussed with her the feeling I got whenever something bad was coming, and it hadn't ever failed me. Ever. Whenever it occurred, something bad always happened.

I got the same feeling when we were in North Carolina. My grandmother had always claimed I was *blessed*. It was something I never believed in, but I did have a gut instinct that told me when shit was about to go down.

"A sense of familiarity hit me, but I thought it was my imagination. I thought maybe I was overacting, so like a fucking idiot, I shrugged the feeling off. I shouldn't have shrugged it off."

"Wait. What are you trying to say, Rey?"

I reached over and picked one of the photos. "Victim number nine. Daniella Strong, age twenty-nine. I remember so much about these women's lives, DeeDee, that it's become second nature recalling their last days."

"I'm so sorry, Rey."

"Nothing to be sorry about. It comes with the job." I shook the picture. "This picture was one of the last photos ever taken of Daniella before she went missing the following day. She never made it to work Monday morning after having brunch with her parents on Sunday. According to her friends, Daniella was the life of the party, and her parents said she was the rock of their family. She'd been missing more than a week before her body turned up in Laurels Bayou attached to victim number ten, twenty-eight-year-old Dawn Ellis." I took in a deep breath and released it. "I will never forget their mothers' wails when Amir and I made the death notification."

I gazed at it for a few more minutes before I handed it to her.

"Look at her, DeeDee. I mean, really look at her. All of them." I motioned to the pictures of all the victims splayed across the bed. "Who do they look like to you? Tell me I'm going fucking crazy."

Her eyes widened when she looked at the picture I handed her. I stalked to the bathroom, grabbed her toiletries, and tossed them in the suitcase. She swallowed hard and crossed her arms over her chest, trying to find an answer to my question that went against the obvious. She knew. No matter how much she denied the truth to herself, I was right, and she knew it.

These dead women were a pawn in a serial killer's game. She was his real target, and I'd led her straight to him like a fucking lamb to the slaughter.

"How could I be so fucking stupid?" I gripped my hair and tugged on it before I dropped my hands, thinking about all the things I needed to do to get ahead of this bastard.

"You can't be serious, Rey."

She held the picture of Daniella out toward me. I took it and looked at it one more time before tossing it on top of the others on the bed.

"You think these women look like me?"

The tremble in her voice tore at my heart, but she needed to look at the situation from a logical standpoint, not an emotional one. She was the best at what she did, so now was the time for her to do that crazy shit she did so well and not be caught up in her emotions.

The bastard had been sending signs…signs I'd fucking missed, but now I understood what he was doing. He'd used me to get her back to Louisiana, from dumping women who looked like her into Laurels Bayou to getting rid of them in my parish. Shit, even all their names started with the same damn letter. It had been about her this entire time, and I had fallen right into his trap.

"They resemble you, DeeDee. Open your eyes." I zipped up her suitcase, grabbed all the files on the case, including the picture of Daniella, and packed them in her briefcase. "Everything this fucker is doing comes back to you. The way these women look, their accomplishments in their professions, even fucking Laurels Bayou. Me, my parish. Their fucking first names all begin with the same letter as yours!"

How could I have been so fucking stupid, bringing her back here?

"What about the Kinbaku then?" She glared at me with her hands on her hips. "I'm not into that, and I don't frequent those types of online sites either."

"I hadn't figured that shit out yet, but I'm sure it's got something to do with you. Maybe the work you did during grad school?" I tossed my hands in the air. "Shit, Dee, I don't fucking know. What I do know is we're going to figure this shit out, at *our* home. Not here. So, let's go."

For a moment, she stood still. Dana was the strongest woman I knew, but the news that all this had something to do with her had shaken her to her core. Like most law enforcement officers, we received death threats weekly. It came along with the job. Dana was a high-profile criminal profiler for the FBI. She was constantly on television during high-profile cases or speaking at law enforcement conferences, so I was sure she'd received her share of threats from nut jobs, not to mention the shit she went through in college with that psycho. But this killer's obsession went beyond the normal stuff we received from crazies. She was the target of an intelligent killer who'd evaded capture for at least eight months, with at least twelve women's deaths attributed to him. All because he wanted her attention.

Over my dead body, would she stay here.

I walked up to her and wrapped her in my arms. "I'm not relenting on this one, sweetheart. You're mine to protect, and I can't do that with you here. You're coming home with me, and that's final."

With a deep sigh, she finally gave in. I didn't know if it was the fear she saw in my eyes, but when she agreed, I relaxed and let out a breath of relief. I wanted control over this situation. As of right now, whoever the killer was had been in control of my every move, including pulling Dana into this. Hopefully, with her under my roof, I could protect her from whatever the killer had planned.

"There's no chance I'll be seeing Chanel there?"

"What the hell is it with you and her?" I asked as I grabbed her suitcases and escorted her out of the hotel room.

"Just answer the damn question, Rey. I do not want to see that woman anywhere near the house while I'm staying there."

When we stepped onto the elevator, I set her suitcases down and pushed the button for the lobby. I took in a deep breath and exhaled. No one on this earth was more important than Dana, and I hated that she couldn't see that. Chanel was a warm body. A warm body I used to relieve stress and forget about her. Chanel was one of many.

I reached out and caressed her face, feeling her smooth, velvety skin against my fingertips. It was one thing I missed, just being able to touch her. Her eyes fluttered.

"DeeDee, for the last time, there is nothing serious going on between Chanel and me. She's nothing more than a piece of ass. No, you will not be seeing her."

She released a breath and nodded.

Why couldn't she see that she was the only one for me?

Chapter Seven

Detective Rey LaCroix

Having Dana back home was strange but welcomed. She hadn't been here since the night she'd left, and I felt a little self-conscious about her being here even though I'd given her no other choice but to come home.

While I hadn't changed a single thing in the place, including our wedding photos still proudly on display, she didn't mention it as she walked through, nor did she mention the photo of us on our first trip together sitting on the nightstand beside our bed, the same place it had been since we'd taken it.

When I offered the master bed for her to sleep in, of course, she fought tooth and nail, but I didn't feel right having her in the same bed I fucked Chanel in. I regretted even tainting that room with Chanel's presence. But, when I finally became exhausted from arguing, I asked if she would rather sleep in the actual bed I fucked her in or the one no other woman had been in except her.

That shut up her protest quick.

"Where are you going to sleep?" she asked as she slid under the covers of our bed while I plugged my phone into the charger beside the bed.

As soon as we'd arrived and got the arguing out of the way, she'd jumped in the shower in the master suite, and I'd used the one in the guest bedroom. Now, all my senses were on high alert. She still used cocoa butter on her lush skin and the same sweet-smelling shampoo.

A mischievous grin touched my face. It had been a long day and night, and now, it was after three in the morning. A couple more homicides added to the ever-growing list of deaths in the parish, and now with the threats against her, I wanted nothing more than to see her smile and have her in my arms.

"Where do you think I'm going to sleep, DeeDee? In *our* bed."

"Rey, this isn't *our* bed. This is *your* bed that you've kindly allowed me to use while I stay here, and I don't think that's such a good idea."

"Why not?"

"What do you mean, why not?"

"You scared you can't keep your hands to yourself?"

A beautiful flush stained her cheeks. She giggled and shook her head. The sound was like music to my ears. I would rather us banter back and forth to keep her mind off the dire situation we were in and the target that had been placed squarely on her back.

"There's that smile. Listen, sweetheart, I just want to hold you in my arms. This shit has my nerves rattled and yours. We were friends before we were lovers, DeeDee. Right now, we both need each other. I need to know my friend is safe. I need to know I'm keeping her safe."

Although her look was skeptical, she agreed. So, I started to remove my t-shirt, then reached for my boxers.

"Wait!" She held her hands up. "Rey, what are you doing?"

I looked at her, confused. She knew I didn't sleep with clothes on, even before we'd married. I loved the feeling of the cold sheets against my skin. It calmed me after long days or nights at the station, and tonight, I needed fucking calm.

"I'm getting ready to go to sleep."

"Rey, you cannot get into this bed without any clothes on."

"It's not like you haven't seen it all before. I've been balls deep in that wet pussy of yours for years, sweetheart."

She scoffed, and I laughed.

"DeeDee, we're both adults. I'm sure you can tamp down your attraction to me long enough to get a few hours of sleep."

"Whatever." She rolled her eyes and turned her back to me, but not before she perused my body.

"Like what you see?" I asked, continuing to laugh.

"Shut up, Rey, and get in the damn bed."

I heard the amusement in her voice.

After sliding off my boxers, I pulled back the covers and slid into bed next to her—the last place I thought she'd ever be again. Although she clearly didn't want to get anywhere near me if her being on the edge of the bed was a sign, there was no way I wouldn't have her in my arms, not with her so close. I wrapped my arms around her midsection, pulling her against my naked body. I nuzzled my nose into her thick, coily hair, sighing.

"I love you, DeeDee."

She tensed but didn't pull away. I kissed her head, and she relaxed against me. I didn't expect a response. I just needed her to know my feelings for her never changed. I never stop loving her. Even when I let her go, she remained in my heart and always would.

She wiggled her hips, and I tightened my embrace to stop her movements, my dick hardening against her luscious ass. "If you don't want me to fuck you senseless," I squeezed her hips, "I suggest you stop rubbing your glorious ass against my cock."

She stopped immediately. "Sorry," she mumbled.

I chuckled. "Get some sleep, DeeDee. We've only got a few hours and an early start."

"Goodnight, Rey," she yawned, "and thanks for being there."

"I'll always be there for you, DeeDee. Always."

And that was the truth. Although I was an asshole when she got her job with the FBI, my loyalty to my wife never wavered. If Dana needed me to slay the biggest motherfucker on the planet, all she had to do was ask. This creep didn't know what I'd do to protect her. Even if it cost me my life, he'd never get his hands on her.

· · · ● · ● · ● · · ·

So soft. So warm.

I snuggled closer, grinding my hips against her soft, plush ass and a lustful moan was my reward. I'd had every intention just to hold her in my arms, but I was beyond my ability not to be inside her. She had the softest skin, the plushest ass, and the lushest tits I'd ever had the pleasure to squeeze.

Damn, I miss her.

With my face in her hair, I inhaled the sweet smell of her shampoo that mingled with the scent of cocoa butter. It was a familiar scent, one I didn't realize I'd missed so much until now.

I slowly moved my hand across her silken stomach under her shirt until I reached her breast, tweaking and pinching her nipple until it became rigid between my fingertips. I remembered how she loved a little pain with pleasure.

"Rey," she moaned.

"Hmm?"

"Wake up."

"I am awake." I bit the soft flesh over her collarbone, and she pushed back against my hardened cock. DeeDee was always so receptive to my touch. "And so is my dick."

She chuckled, looking over her shoulder at me. "If we don't stop this now," she said, wiggling her hips, causing me to groan as the sensation moved across my body, "we'll make a huge mistake."

I quickly rolled her on her back, pushed her legs open with my knee, and settled between her luscious thighs with my palms planted on either side of her head. I saw the longing in her eyes. She wanted me, but fear also mingled with her desire for me.

"What are you scared of, baby?" I moved strands of hair out of her face. "It's me."

She turned her head away, focusing on anything but me. I gripped her chin, forcing her to look at me. I needed to understand why she was afraid and why her beautiful brown eyes were glassy from unshed tears.

"I'm not scared of you, Rey." She sighed. "I'm scared of getting hurt by you. Nothing has changed. I still have my job in Atlanta, and you still have your job here in the parish. Are you willing to leave?"

Was I?

"I don't know what the future holds for us, DeeDee, but what I do know is I love you with all my heart. That's never changed. Any time with you like this would never be a mistake, and I'm not letting you go this time. We'll figure it out."

"You make it sound so easy."

She chuckled while tears slipped from her eyes. My heart ached, knowing I was the reason for them.

"My heart can't take it again, Rey."

"I'm not here to hurt you, DeeDee." I took the pad of my thumb and wiped her tears. "I'm here to love you like I have since the first day I met you."

Her gaze bore into my soul, searching for the truth. She'd find all she needed to know as long as she looked. I wore my heart on my sleeve, but only with her. There were no lies between us, *ever*. She released a breath, and I took that as my cue to move forward. Yearning swam in her eyes, and I was sure the same was reflected in mine.

"I want you, DeeDee, but if you're not ready, I can wait." I trailed my fingers down her cheek. "I can wait as long as you need me to."

"I want you too," she responded without hesitation, cupping my face. "I've wanted you for the past three years. I've missed you so damn much."

She didn't need to say anymore, and my calm was completely shattered when her soft lips caressed mine. Her sigh of contentment stirred something deep within me. For three years, I'd longed to hear her breathless moans and screams of ecstasy, and now that it was happening, there was no way I would let her go after this. Dana LaCroix was mine again. She would be in my life and bed permanently from this day forward. I'd see to it.

I deepened our kiss. It had been so long since we'd been like this, I couldn't hold back. Tender and sweet would be something to have later, but right now, I needed to sink into her wet warm pussy and fuck her until she was hoarse from screaming my name.

I pulled her T-shirt over her head, then snatched off her black lace panties, which had taunted me all morning, and tossed them over my shoulder, causing her to laugh.

"Condom?" she asked, her voice sultry and laced with lust.

Her request briefly threw me for a loop. We'd never used them before, and she had always been on the pill, but she was also right. For three long fucking years, we'd lived separate lives, and I didn't want to think about who she screwed. I'd had my share of one-night stands after drunken nights at *Lucky's* if I didn't call Chanel to fill the urge. I wouldn't put her life at risk, even though I never fucked anyone without strapping up.

I nodded and reached for the nightstand on my side of the bed, taking the black foil packet from the drawer, tearing it with my teeth before rolling it on. While I'd love nothing more than to fuck her skin-to-skin, it would have to wait. As soon as we were tested and cleared, these would be thrown in the trash. I needed to feel all of her.

After I settled back between her thighs, my demanding lips caressed hers—still warm and moist from our earlier kiss. "I've missed you, DeeDee." My mouth brushed against hers as I spoke. "I've missed you so much, sweetheart."

It was ecstasy when she returned my kiss with such unadulterated passion. Although she hadn't said the words, her kiss told me every-thing—she'd missed me just as much. My hand seared a path down her stomach onto her thigh, gripping her soft flesh. Her legs widened further, and I swiftly entered while holding her hands above her head with my other hand. We both groaned at the sensation. My tongue caressed her swollen nipples while I continued to thrust into her.

"Rey," she moaned, "please."

She wrapped her legs around my waist as I continued to thrust in and out of her warm, wet pussy.

"Please what, baby?" I bit her bottom lip. "Say it, and I'll give it to you."

She lifted her hips, and I went deeper, so deep it was hard holding back the orgasm trying its damndest to rip through me. I shifted to my knees, lifting her hips higher, before rubbing her clit.

"Is this what you want, DeeDee?" I asked, although I wasn't expecting any answer.

Her eyes rolled back before closing, and her body arched toward me. With her legs wrapped tightly around my waist, I pounded her relentlessly as she fisted the bedsheets, begging me to go faster and harder. The walls of her slick pussy fluttered around my cock, sending a euphoric sensation across my entire body and pushing me closer to the edge than I would've liked, but there was nothing I could do about it. I'd been away from her too long, and I'd always been addicted to every moan, every sigh, and every scream DeeDee made.

I dug my fingers into her hips as her body writhed under me, loving the sounds of her voice and the smell of our lovemaking that filled the room.

"Rey, I'm coming!" she yelled, her tight pussy clenching my dick after I twisted her hardened nipples, sending her soaring.

It never failed. Over the years with DeeDee, I'd learned the ways of her magnificent body, and all it took was a little pain to her nipples, and she'd scream my name.

"Shit!" I groaned, pushed into her deeper, and released into the condom.

Reluctantly, I slipped from inside her, removed the condom, then disposed of it in the wastebasket beside the nightstand. When I lay back in the bed, pulling her limp, sweaty frame closer to mine, she sighed, and I kissed the top of her head. We lay in silence, waiting for our breathing to return to normal. The sun peeked through the curtains.

It was time for us to return to reality.

A killer was after her, but for a few minutes at least, we'd been able to get lost in our love for one another, and it would be a moment I'd cherish until I took my last breath. I'd lost her once before, and I refused to do it again.

"I love you, DeeDee."

She relaxed further into my body, wrapping my arm tighter around her middle. "I love you too, Rey."

If I hadn't been so content being wrapped around her body, I would've gotten up and done a damn dance. Even though I knew she still loved me, I hadn't about thought of how the words would affect me when she finally said them—if she ever said them again. I'd missed hearing it.

"We only have a few minutes before Amir shows up," I mumbled against the hair.

She sighed, and I understood exactly how she felt. I wished we could stay this way, at least for the day before the shit hit the fan, but we couldn't because a madman had his eyes on her.

"You take the master bathroom," I pecked her on the lips before sliding out of bed, "and I'll take the guest."

"Why don't you take the master bathroom with me?" she asked, standing.

I perused her naked body. Nothing had really changed other than her hips were a little wider and her thighs a little thicker. Damn, she was exquisite.

"Because if we take a shower together, we're not coming out any time soon."

"And what's so wrong with that?" she replied, walking toward the bathroom with a little more sway in her hips.

I groaned, licking my lips at the gorgeous sight of her round ass. My cock hardened, and I stroked it as she looked over her shoulder.

"Amir can wait," I mumbled and rushed over to her as she dashed into the bathroom, laughing.

I couldn't wait until this was all over. There was no way Dana was going back to her life without me in it.

Chapter Eight

The Infinity Killer

One...two...three...four...want him dead.

I pounded the sides of my head, then pulled on the curly strands of my hair to get them to quiet down so I could focus.

Kill him...kill him. SHE IS OURS!

"Shut the fuck up!" I paced just out of sight, seething, watching the love of my life fuck another man through the open blinds. "I can't fucking think when all of you are talking at one time."

FOUR will not be quiet. SHE IS OURS...kill him! Take her! Take her now!

"Shut up for just one minute," I growled through clenched teeth. "One minute of silence so I can fucking breathe. So, I can think."

I wanted to take her, and *they* were right. She was ours, but I had to be careful now that she was back. I let her know it was time for her to come home so we could spend eternity together. Trying to get her attention was tiresome. These bitches only wanted the pleasure my rope provided, but all I wanted was her. Now, it was time to take what was mine.

You're a fucking idiot. You let him take her. Now he's fucking what is OURS!

"Shut up! I know what I'm doing!"

In a few hours, I would put our plan into motion.

Fuck the plan! Take her! She is ours!

They wouldn't stop talking until it was done, but I needed to stay strong.

"Stick to the plan, Harold. Stick to the plan."

The other cop I despised, Amir Shaw, pulled up at the perfect time. Although I had no problem with him, he would be the key to getting Dana. I followed his every move, trying to find the perfect opportunity to strike. Now was definitely the time.

"Let's get this show on the road."

Yes...yes. It's time. Take her! Take her!

· · · **·** · **·** · · ·

She was such a beautiful woman. I ran my finger down her jawline. Right complexion, similar features. The hair wasn't the same, but close enough.

"Such a fucking waste."

Just do it! Why wait? One...Two...Three...Four...do not want her. She looks like OURS, but she's just like the rest.

"Stop talking!" I screamed, my voice echoing off the cinderblock walls of the basement. I hoped they would obey for once. I couldn't work when they talked to me. Too distracting. Too much pressure. She may end up like the rest.

Her eyes remained closed despite my outburst. Silence. Just what I liked. She was silent, and so were they.

Her plump lips, I wanted to taste. Her beautiful pussy, I wanted to fuck. But I restrained myself. I had a job to do.

I took the jute rope and weaved it around her body, tightly binding her curvy frame to perfection. When she woke, she wouldn't be able to move due to the bindings, and the paralytic I gave her wouldn't allow her to speak.

Precious silence.

My cock hardened at the thought.

Forty-five minutes later, I finished the pattern, weaving the infinity symbol with the ropes at the end. All that was missing was *her*.

Her eyes fluttered, and I clapped my hands, excited for what was next.

Great! She's waking up.

I brushed a strand of her coily hair away from her face, and her eyes popped open. They weren't like Dana's, but none of the women's eyes were. They were all replacements for the real thing.

Fear and tears filled her beautiful dark eyes. Exactly what I craved. I closed my eyes, relishing in the shiver of pleasure running down my spine.

I pulled my cock from my jeans and fisted it, the red tip already glistening. She squeezed her eyes shut, and a tear trickled down her beautiful dark skin, sending a sensation straight through me. Pumping my cock, I relished in the power and excitement moving through me.

"Don't worry, sweetheart." I licked her tears away. "You're not the one I'm after, but you'll help me get her."

Her tears fell faster, and I fucking loved it. My eyes rolled back, and fire rose from the soles of my feet and covered my entire body in nothing but pure bliss as my orgasm took over.

"Dana," I whispered while ropes of cum landed on my hand and the concrete floor.

I took a deep breath, opened my eyes, and focused on the beautiful, terrified woman in front of me. I pushed my cock inside my pants and walked over to the table sitting against one of the walls of my basement. I picked up a couple of wet wipes, walked back to the woman, wiped her face clean of my saliva, then cleaned my hands and tossed them in the metal trash bin sitting beside the table.

I thought about what I wanted to do first. She was already prepared, and it was only a matter of time before they knew she was missing. But I was tired of waiting. I needed Dana now.

I walked back to the woman restrained so beautifully. I could only imagine how sexy the natural fibers of the jute would look against Dana's skin.

"Shall we get ready?" I asked, picking up the burner phone and dialing the police department.

I waited, fingering a coil of the woman's hair. After the third ring, someone finally answered.

Chapter Nine

Dr. Dana LaCroix

"Rey, I don't believe this is necessary. I'm your consultant, not a victim," I complained as he walked me into his precinct headquarters.

Of course, after Amir had shown up this morning with news that the hotel security footage was a bust, Rey had insisted I come along with him to the office. No matter how much I told him it was ridiculous and that I was safe at home, he refused to budge.

"We have to let Cap know, Dana," he squeezed my hand, "especially since you have no choice but to inform the higher-ups in the FBI that one of their own is being targeted by a serial killer."

He was right. I hated to admit it and didn't like being classified as a victim. All those girls were dead because of me. I wasn't a victim. They were.

"Well, if it isn't Dana LaCroix," Captain Broussard said as soon as we made it through the lobby to Rey's desk. "Long time no see, beautiful."

"Hey, Broussard," I replied, giving him a kiss on the cheek. "How's Marilyn?"

"Bitching as usual."

I laughed as he rolled his eyes. One thing about Broussard was that he absolutely hated his wife. Everyone knew he was only with the woman because she had money, and he wanted to retire; he couldn't do so on a cop's salary. So, Marilyn's money was his ticket to rest and relaxation on the beaches of Florida, despite how many times he complained about being married to her for thirty-plus years.

"So, you finally decided to give this asshole another chance?" he asked, motioning to Rey.

"Actually, we both need to speak to you in private, Cap," Rey said and the Cap's face turned serious.

I was relieved at the interruption. I had no idea what was happening between us, and I didn't want to share information with anyone about our new situation.

The captain narrowed his eyes but motioned for us to follow him to his office. "Close the door." He gestured to the seats in front of his desk. "What's going on?"

"We've had a breakthrough with the serial killer case," Rey said as we sat in front of Captain Broussard's desk.

"We?" He planted his forearms on his desk and glared at Rey. "Detective LaCroix, this police department has not requested the FBI's help. We don't need the FBI's help with a serial killer case because we don't have a serial killer in the parish."

"Well, Cap, I'm sorry, but the FBI is involved," Rey said. "The killer is targeting DeeDee."

He leaned back, his office chair squeaking under his weight. "How is the FBI involved in local matters, Detective LaCroix," he rubbed his temples, "especially when we haven't released any information?"

"Rey asked for my help," I replied. "As a personal consultant."

"As a personal consultant," the captain repeated in anger, his face tinting red, a vein bulging at the center of his forehead.

"Before you blow a gasket, Cap, I did what was necessary. Without officially getting the FBI involved, I went to DeeDee for help to get insight into this guy. We couldn't get shit on him. What did you expect me to do?" Rey said, throwing his hands up in the air in frustration. "I knew DeeDee could help!"

Broussard stood, slamming his palms on the desk. "It wasn't your place to go to your ex-wife about this case."

"So, you'd rather these girls keep dying on our watch?" Rey shouted before he took a calming breath. "Look, Cap, I did what I thought was best."

Broussard sat down and released a breath of his own. "You know the *Brass* is going to have a big fucking problem with this, LaCroix. Find a way to spin it."

"He's targeting me, Broussard." I placed my hands against my chest. "Me. A Behavioral Analyst for the FBI. What other way do you need to spin it? Now you can get the FBI involved officially because my superiors *have to* be notified that a killer is targeting me."

"Cap, these women are carbon copies of DeeDee," Rey said, continuing to plead his case to Broussard. "He's targeting my wife."

"Ex-wife," Broussard countered, steepling his hands.

"My wife," Rey argued.

The beginnings of a smile tipped the corners of my mouth. Even though we'd been divorced for three years, he still considered me his wife.

Broussard sighed. "Call in your team, Dana."

Rey stood, and I followed. "Thanks, Cap."

He held up his hand. "Don't fucking thank me yet." He pointed at Rey. "If this goes to hell, LaCroix, it's your badge."

"I'm prepared for that."

"I hope the fuck you are because that's how all this will end. Now get the hell out of my office."

"Thank you, Broussard," I said.

He waved his hand, dismissing me.

Stepping out of the captain's office, I took a breath. Rey and Amir were good at their jobs, but with the help of the FBI, the extra eyes couldn't hurt.

And maybe I won't die.

"Rey! Rey!" Amir called out, motioning for Rey to come to where their desks were located. His hand covered the receiver of the landline phone on his desk as he frantically waved Rey over. I followed Rey and sat at his desk while Rey grabbed the phone from Amir.

"Put it on speaker," Amir whispered.

Rey nodded, hit the speaker button, then set the receiver down. "Detective LaCroix."

"Tick-Tock, Detective. Tick-Tock. Your time is running out."

The voice was a strained, southern accent, but not Louisiana southern. Maybe North or South Carolina.

"Excuse me?" Rey asked.

"Trade one for another before the clock strikes midnight," the mysterious caller said.

"What the hell are you talking about?" Rey shouted. The tension rolled off him. "Who is this?"

"She'll die at midnight unless you give me Dana, detective."

Rey stared at me. My eyes widened, and I mouthed *'the killer'* to him. He nodded.

"Who will die?" Rey asked.

"Ask Detective Shaw. Does he know where his wife is?"

"You son of a bitch!" Rey shouted before dead air replaced the southern accent on the line.

Amir fumbled for his cell phone and dialed Delaney's number. Concern, fear, and anger clouded his eyes as he gripped the phone tightly in his hands while he paced.

He ended the call and dialed it again.

Delaney was Black and around my height with tightly-coiled dark brown hair. We were mistaken for sisters often. Her name began with the letter D, like mine, and she was on the board of executives at the local hospital. She fit the victim profile perfectly.

While Amir worked to get Delaney on the phone, Rey informed Captain Broussard about the phone call and Delaney's possible disappearance. I pulled my phone from my purse and dialed Mr. Steele's number while they managed things on their end.

"This is Mr. Steele's office. My name is Stacey. How may I help you?"

I hated to get the FBI involved. There was always a pissing match between the agency and the locals, and this time would be no different. There was no way Rey would give up control of this case, especially since I was the target, and Delaney had been kidnapped. This wasn't going to go over well with my superiors.

"Hello, Stacey." I sighed. "It's Dr. LaCroix."

"Hello, Dr. LaCroix. How may I help you?"

"I need to speak with Mr. Steele, immediately."

I watched Amir storm out of the precinct. Rey's head dropped, and his fists clenched at his sides. Anguish marred his features, and at that moment, I understood how much I wanted to make all his troubles go away. It had always been me and Rey against the world. We were going to make a difference. Now, it was up to me to get Delaney back.

"Dr. LaCroix, I didn't expect to hear from you on your vacation. How can I help you?"

"Mr. Steele, we have a problem, and you're not going to like it."

He sighed. "I'm listening."

I wasn't sure he'd even send a team from Atlanta, but I was sure the FBI field office in Louisiana would be involved. Any help would be good.

Chapter Ten

Detective Rey LaCroix

The only time I remembered experiencing fear like this was when I realized Dana had really left me and that she wasn't coming back. Now, once again, the fear of losing her overwhelmed me. I had lived three years without her while she lived her life in Atlanta, and it had crippled me. I still had trouble with her being gone. Now, the thought that she might be taken away from me by a crazy killer sent absolute dread through me.

I paced the length of the living room while the Feds from the Atlanta field office fit Dana with a wire. My hair was now unruly from constantly running my hands through it due to the fear that gripped me in a tight hold. According to their tech guy, the wire was untraceable, so there was no way the killer would be able to spot it. I wasn't so sure, but I had to trust they'd keep her safe, and trusting anybody other than myself for that job wasn't an easy thing to do.

"She's the best at what she does." A deep male's voice stopped me in my tracks.

Agent Aaron Hart. Her lover.

Closing my eyes, I pinched the bridge of my nose as anger barreled through me. "I don't need you telling me a goddamn thing about *my* wife."

Although I had no right to be angry with Agent Hart, it was impossible not to be. Days, nights, and achievements, as well as her disappointments that should have been shared with me, were shared with him. It wasn't his fault. I had been an asshole. The fault was all mine, but he was a reminder of what I'd given up. A reminder I certainly didn't want when the love of my life was walking into the fucking hands of a murderer.

"Ex-wife." He said it with such confidence, it caused me to snap.

My head snapped to him, and all the rage for him and their relationship surged forward. To know he'd experienced just a little bit of what I had with her caused my blood to boil.

"Fuck you!"

When my fist connected with his jaw, all hell broke loose. He gave just as good as he got. We broke furniture, smashed vases, and crushed my glass coffee table, but none of it mattered. Agent Hart represented what I'd given up, and I wanted to end him.

Hands grabbed at him and me as we were pulled apart.

"What the hell is wrong with you two?" Dana screamed, pushing against our chests as she stood between us.

Agent Hart shook out of the other agent's hold and wiped the blood from his nose with the back of his hand, smearing blood across his cheek as he glared at me. I wiped the blood from my mouth with the pad of my thumb.

"My friend is in the hands of a killer, and you two want to have a pissing contest!" She looked between the two of us like we weren't shit. And we weren't. I'd let my anger get the best of me.

"DeeDee…"

"Dana…"

We called out to her in unison.

"Save it!" She threw her hands up at the both of us. "I don't want to hear shit from either of you." She stormed out of the living room to our bedroom, the door slamming behind her.

My hands went to my hips, and I sighed. I caught sight of Agent Hart being led outside by one of the other agents who'd arrived from the Atlanta Field Office.

After I calmed myself down, I made my way to our bedroom. Cautiously, I opened the door. Dana was sitting on the edge of the bed with her head in her hands, and my heart ached. I'd caused her so much pain over the years, and it looked like I couldn't stop myself from doing it again.

"I'm sorry, DeeDee."

She looked up at me with bloodshot eyes, and my heart squeezed inside my chest.

"What did you expect when I left, Rey? Did you expect me to put my life on pause? Or did you expect me to come back saying I made a mistake by leaving you?"

I sat beside her on the bed and planted my forearms on my knees. "Honestly, I didn't expect to have to fight for you, DeeDee." I blew out a breath. "When you left, I always expected you to come back."

"Of course you did. You arrogant ass. Our relationship was always about what you wanted, never about me. In the beginning, instead of you offering to upend your life and move to North Carolina, you expected me to run to you. And I did. Everything in my life, I've done for you, but when it came to me and my career, you expected me to give all of it up for you."

"You're right, and I'm sorry."

"Sorry." She scoffed. "Do you think sorry fixes this?"

"What do you expect me to say, DeeDee?" I ran my hand down my face. "I'm an asshole. You know it, and so do I. I disregarded your needs and your dreams for what I wanted."

She stared at me like I'd grown another head, which made me feel even more shitty about the person I'd been back then. I was an asshole. Had taken her for granted. I hadn't seen it until she was gone, but I recognized it now. I was lost without her.

I'm still lost without her.

"When I got those papers," I continued, hoping to make her understand the headspace I'd been in back then, "you made it perfectly clear you wanted that job. I thought I had no right to interfere with your career. You never interfered in mine, and for the first time in our relationship, I needed to put you first."

"I was willing to work something out, Rey. You were my husband. And that still doesn't explain why you immediately started fucking Chanel since, according to you, you still loved me. That's not love, Rey."

My brows furrowed. "Yes, I started fucking Chanel, but almost a year later. I always thought we still had a chance, then as more time passed, I didn't know anymore. You were moving on with your life with that asshole."

"Rey, Aaron is a great guy."

I threw up my hand. "I know I have no right to be angry, but you looked so happy without me. You looked so happy with him, and it pissed me the fuck off."

"And Chanel let me know how happy you were without me, too." She rolled her eyes.

"I don't know what you heard or who you heard it from, but Chanel isn't as important to me as you're making her out to be. She's not even the only woman I've fucked since we split!"

She rolled her eyes again. "I don't need to hear the details of your sex life, Rey."

A knock sounded at the door before I could respond, causing both of us to groan. Chanel was keeping us separated. She shouldn't be, but she was. We were going to have to tackle that problem in order to take the next step.

I walked to the door and yanked it open. "Yes?"

"Detective, I'm sorry to interrupt, but we're running out of time. I need to make sure all the communications are working," the tech guy said.

"Okay, we'll be out in a minute."

He gave a curt nod and walked back down the hallway. I shut the door and faced Dana. "Are you sure about this?"

"I can't let him hurt anyone else, Rey."

I walked toward her and stopped inches in front of her.

"Not because of me," she said.

I grabbed her arms, pulling her up from the bed. "If anything seems out of the ordinary, you get out of there, you hear me? We'll find Delaney another way."

"I love you, Rey."

She ignored my comment, but I wouldn't call her on it. Dana would do whatever she could to save Delaney, even if that meant sacrificing herself, but I wouldn't let anything happen to her. I refused to lose her again.

"I love you too, sweetheart."

I kissed her lips and fought the urge to deepen it. I forced myself to pull back. Even though it felt like a goodbye, I wouldn't let it be. I would die to protect her. Even if it was my last day on this earth, it wouldn't be hers.

Chapter Eleven

Dr. Dana LaCroix

Immediately, a chill ran down my spine. The hairs on the back of my neck and arms stood on end. He was here, hiding, waiting amongst the weekend crowd. I shook off the unnerving feeling and slid onto the only empty stool at the worn, wooden L-shaped bar of *Lucky's Dive.*

The same dusty, red and white, saucer-shaped hanging lights dimly lit the smoke-filled bar. I hadn't been here in years, and nothing had really changed. The same vintage Coca-Cola sign Rey had picked up at an estate sale in Charlotte then gave to Lucky still hung on the wood wall beside the hallway leading to the stock room, Lucky's office, and the bathrooms. The same photo of Lucky, Rey, and blues legend, Buddy Guy that I had taken for Lucky's seventy-fifth birthday still hung proudly behind the bar, among others.

While Lucky, the previous owner, had passed away a year before I left town, it remained the same. The only thing missing was Lucky's voice crooning old tunes from a blues legend he'd met at one time or another in his life. I used to love listening to his stories whenever Rey and I stopped by.

Hidden among the bald cypress forests covered in Spanish moss, *Lucky's Dive* sat at the end of a long dirt road, right off one of Louisiana's many bayous in the middle of nowhere. If you weren't a local, you'd never be able to find the place, even if someone gave you directions. That was why it wasn't a place that tourists frequented unless they came with a local. And it couldn't be just any local, but someone born and raised here.

So, this guy's a local, or he's been following me a lot longer than we thought.

It was information I wanted to give Rey, but I couldn't risk the killer seeing me speaking.

"Okay, DeeDee," Rey said through the earpiece in my ear. "I'm right here with you, okay?"

The gadget was so small it was non-detectable to the naked eye. It was comforting to hear his voice, but it was still terrifying to know someone was coming after you, with no explanation for the where, why, or even who that person was or why you were even chosen.

"Blood and Sand for the lady," the bartender said with a smile as he set the drink in front of me.

"Shit!" Rey said.

My favorite drink.

Only those close to me knew this used to be my favorite drink, and only those who were close to me knew I hadn't had a drink since my college years and why.

"Um, I didn't order this." I pushed the drink back to the bartender, who couldn't have been more than twenty-two. Most likely a college student just trying to survive.

"I know, ma'am." He jerked his thumb toward the end of the bar. "The man at the end of the bar did."

"Who?" I asked as I looked at an empty barstool.

"Hmm..." The bartender shrugged. "He's not there anymore."

"Can you describe what he looks like?"

The young man wiped his blond hair out of his eyes. "Hmmm...let me see. Blond hair but darker than mine. Bright green eyes. Thin. Scruffy beard. Mid-thirties. Southern accent, but not from around here southern. That's all I got."

"Thank you," I said.

He walked off to the other side of the bar, and I discreetly looked around the room. I didn't see anyone who fit that description, but I knew he was here somewhere. He wouldn't leave until he got me.

"Rey, did you hear any of that?" I whispered, hoping the wire picked up my voice. I did my best to hide my mouth.

"Who...i..t?" Rey asked in my ear, but his voice was coming in and out.

I focused on the room once more. I wasn't alone in here. Two more agents were discreetly placed around the room, but I think this guy was too smart to bite. Although he'd told me to come alone, he knew there was no chance of that.

Feeling eyes on me, I zeroed in on the long, narrow hallway at the back of the bar leading to the stock room, office, and bathrooms. A man standing in the doorway smiled. Familiarity hit me instantly, and then fear. It couldn't be him.

I slipped off the barstool and made my way toward the hallway. I made eye contact with one of the agents. He stared but made no acknowledgment of me. Heading in the stranger's direction, he quickly turned away and disappeared farther down the hallway into the darkness. I entered the room I thought he'd entered, which was Lucky's office. I had expected to see him waiting for me, but he wasn't. The last person I'd expected sat on the edge of Lucky's desk like she didn't have a care in the world.

She hadn't changed since the last time I'd seen her. She still looked like she was one step away from the street.

"Well, look what the cat dragged in," she said, her smile sinister.

Hate was a strong word, but she hated me more than I realized. Was I surprised to see her? No. She always popped up whenever I was in town. Her being here tonight was no different.

"Chanel, I don't have time for this." I turned to walk out.

"You make time unless you want Delaney to die."

I released the doorknob and faced her as shock barreled through my system.

"You had something to do with this?" I asked, taking a step toward her. If I could get close enough, I could take her down. "Where is she, you stupid bitch?"

"Dee...there...we...can't..." Rey's voice came through the earpiece again, but it was still going in and out, and I had to assume he couldn't hear me, either. This wasn't good.

The office door opened. I whipped around, expecting to see one of the agents but instead saw the man I hadn't ever expected to see again. A primal fear shook my body as he took a step toward me.

"Hello, Dana." He took another step forward while I took steps back to get as far away from him as I could until I bumped into Chanel. The smirk across his face caused my stomach to drop to my feet. "It's time to go."

I gasped at the sharp pain in my neck, and my vision blurred. "Wha...who..."

I grabbed at the spot. My body became so heavy that I couldn't stand under my own power anymore and crumpled to the floor. "Rey...help..." I tried to cry out, but the words came out slurred and jumbled.

"How do you plan to get her out of here?" Chanel asked as my eyes drooped.

"Don't worry about that. Just make sure the agent heading this way is occupied."

The voices finally faded, along with my vision, as darkness consumed me.

Chapter Twelve

Detective Rey LaCroix

I shouldn't have waited. I shouldn't have let them hold me back from going to her. I knew as soon as the communication devices started fucking up, something was wrong. I should have gone with my gut.

"Where is she?" I asked, pacing the interrogation room. Not only did we not know where Delaney was, he had Dana too.

"Where's who, baby?"

The sound of her voice tore at my nerves. It was like nails moving down a goddamn chalkboard. Once upon a time, I would've thought twice about putting my hands on a woman, but now, I imagined my hands squeezing Chanel's thin neck until her bones crushed under the weight.

"Chanel, don't fucking play with me!"

Agent Hart stepped between us, slightly pushing me back before I could reach her. "This is not helping Dana." He pushed me back against the wall, pointing his finger in my face. "If you can't get your shit together, then fucking leave, and I'll find her my goddamn self."

It was hard to agree with him, but he was right. Wasting time blowing up at Chanel was a minute longer DeeDee had to spend with that psychopath. A minute longer she was away from me.

I took in a calming breath, then exhaled and pushed his hand off me and his finger out of my face. "I'm good."

I walked around Agent Hart, pulled the chair from under the table, and sat, hoping the table between us would keep me from killing her before I found out any information. "Why are you doing this, Chanel?"

"Doing what, baby?" She tilted her head and smiled. "Fighting for what's mine?" The smirk on her face made me pause. I'd brought this person into our lives. If anything happened to Dana, I didn't know how I'd forgive myself.

"As long as that bitch is in the picture," she continued, "you'll never let her go. So, when he came to me, I agreed to help."

She shrugged like we weren't discussing a human life. Like we weren't discussing the love of my life. But now, I recognized the unhinged look in Chanel's eyes. Everything Dana said about her was front and center now. What I had thought had been a harmless obsession went way beyond that. I could see it now, but now might be too late.

"He approached you?" I asked.

"Yes. Asked if I needed help getting her out of the picture. Why wouldn't I agree to that?" She looked at me like I was the crazy one for not understanding. "You're mine, and she was keeping you from me."

"Who is he?" Agent Hart asked from behind me.

He was propped against the wall of the interrogation room with his arms crossed over his chest.

"Oh! It's you? You love her too, don't you?" She smiled at Agent Hart then focused back on me. "How does this bitch do it? I just don't understand why everyone loves her so much. If she'd never come along, you would have married me, Rey."

Tears gathered in her eyes. There was no fucking way I would have ever married Chanel Boudreaux. There was nothing special about what we shared. She was beyond delusional if she thought because we fucked, we had something special.

"Chanel…"

"Don't." She angrily wiped her tears away. "Don't look at me like that. I'm not crazy, Rey! Everyone in this fucking parish pities me. The poor girl from the other side of the bayou. The orphan. The one nobody wanted. But you did, didn't you, Rey?"

I gritted my teeth. "I did," I lied, and the smile that stretched across her face made me want to vomit. "And now I need your help, Chanel. Who is he?"

"If I tell you, can you promise me you'll give me a chance?" she asked with hope in her eyes. "A real chance."

"I will, Chanel. A real chance," I lied without any hesitation. If it meant I could save DeeDee, I'd tell her whatever she fucking wanted to hear.

"Gary Sutton," she said.

My brows furrowed. "Where have I heard that name?" I mumbled to myself. I pulled out my notepad from my pocket then frantically flipped through the pages.

"What is it, LaCroix?" Agent Hart asked.

"The name." I continued to flip through the notepad. "I know the name. I just don't know where from."

I scanned my notes. "Goddamn it!" I shouted, jerked to my feet, then rushed to the door with Agent Hart on my heels.

"Rey!" Chanel shouted. "Rey! Don't leave me here! I helped you!"

I ignored her pleas and hurried out the door to my desk. "Can you get me everything you have on a Gary Sutton, thirty-four-year-old, white male, divorced, father of two, originally from North Carolina, but moved to Louisiana around seven years ago?" I asked Agent Hart. "He found two of the missing women from our case. We did a deep dive on him, and everything came back squeaky clean, so the name must be an alias."

"You got it," Agent Hart said, whipping out his cell phone.

I paced while he did whatever he could do. The FBI had more resources than we did, so hopefully, we could get a usable lead on this guy. Who the hell was this guy, and why the hell was he so fixated on Dana?

"We got him," Agent Hart said, stopping me in my tracks. "The name is Harold Greely. All the information he gave you was factual, except the name was an alias. I'm waiting on a location."

"I can't fucking believe it." I ran my hand through my hair. "It can't be. What in the hell is he doing out?"

"You know this guy?" Agent Hart asked.

"Yes. The short version is Harold Greely attended the same college as DeeDee. He was a suspect in a string of rapes that terrorized the campus for almost a year. He became fixated on her and spiked her drink at a party. She was able to escape him, and Greely was sentenced to twenty years in a mental facility."

"She never said anything to me about that."

Agent Hart said it more to himself than to me, but his eyes spoke more than words ever could. DeeDee had kept one of the most important pieces of her life from him. I could see why he'd question what part he really played in her life if he didn't know one of the most important pieces that made her who she was. That had put her on the path to becoming a part of the FBI. In the beginning, she'd wanted to learn what made criminals do what they did, but when she became a victim, it shifted her focus. She wanted to be a voice for those who hadn't survived like she had.

"Did you know I wanted to marry her?" he asked, like he was distracted. "But she was never fully in it with me. We were always on one minute, then we'd go our separate ways. She could never let you go."

"I don't want to hear about what you two had together, Hart. All I want to do is find her."

Thank God his phone rang before we could continue the conversation. He held up his index finger while he took the call. I shifted from foot to foot, waiting to see if they'd tracked Harold's location.

Agent Hart ended the call, and the smile that crossed his face caused relief to encompass me. "We've got two addresses. We're sending in two teams. One to each address."

"Which is more secluded?" I asked.

There was no way a person who'd abducted and killed women would do it out in the open. So, he'd more than likely taken Dana to the most secluded location.

"It's about eight miles from your killing field, according to our intelligence," Agent Hart said.

"Then that's the one I'm going to."

CHAPTER THIRTEEN

DR. DANA LACROIX

DANA, DO YOU TAKE Rey to be your lawfully wedded husband to have and to hold from this day forward until death do you part?

I do.

Rey, do you take Dana to be your lawfully wedded wife to have and to hold from this day forward, until death do you part?

I do.

By the power vested in me and the State of North Carolina, I now pronounce you husband and wife. You may kiss the bride.

"One of the best days of my life," I mumbled, my throat dry and scratchy. I tried to swallow, but it was difficult because of the pressure against my neck. I tried to grab at whatever it was, but I was unable to move my arms. "Where the hell am I?"

"DeeDee...DeeDee..."

I groaned, my brain pounding against my skull. "Rey?"

"It's Delaney," she whisper-yelled. "You have to wake up before he comes back."

I blinked a few times to clear my blurred vision, trying to get my bearings. It was kind of hard with the pounding in my head.

"Delaney?" I groaned, the pain ricocheting through me relentlessly. "Is that you?"

"Yes, it's me," she whispered. "We've got to get out of here."

"Where are we?" I asked, not sure if the answer would help us escape, because he had us.

Harold Greely. The person who'd haunted my days and nights had us, and I knew he wouldn't let me go again. I thought I'd never have to deal with him again. He shouldn't have even been out.

Now, everything made sense. The use of Kinbaku. We had studied that in class together, before he'd done what he'd done to me. He was fixated on me now because I was the only one who got away. The only one he didn't get the chance to assault because, according to him, we were in love and would be together intimately on our wedding night. I used what he did to me to make me a better person. To become the person I was today. Harold Greely would not take that away from me.

"I don't know," Delaney said, sighing. "He attacked me when I was coming home from my shift. Thank God Amara was with my mother."

Musty air, along with the strong odor of bleach and ammonia, filled my nostrils. I focused on the bare light bulb with a pull string hanging from the ceiling, then on the small grimy window that barely allowed any light inside to highlight the dark room. The murmur of footsteps overhead filtered down through the open ceiling, which had pipes running along them.

"Can you move?" I asked, pulling at the binds holding me still. I hissed as the fibers of the rope rubbed against my skin.

Jute.

I was completely naked, but my body had been bound with rope, with my lower half on display.

"No. My wrists and ankles are raw," Delaney said.

"Has he hurt you?"

"No, not yet. He's stripped me of all my clothes, and he's done disgusting things, but he hasn't touched me...yet."

I let out a breath of relief. I knew this was something she would have to deal with for the rest of her life, but hearing he hadn't raped her gave me a little relief.

"What does he want with us?"

"He wants me," I said. "Not you. I'm going to get you out of here."

But first, I've got to figure out how.

He didn't want her. Maybe I could use his connection with me to convince him to let her go, then I'd deal with what came after. As long as no one else died because of me, I'd do whatever I had to do.

"Hey!" I screamed at the top of my lungs. "Harold!"

"What are you doing?" Delaney hissed.

The footsteps overhead stopped.

"I'm getting you out of here."

The footsteps started up again, getting closer to where we were tied to metal tables. "DeeDee!" Delaney called out, fear and panic in her voice, but I couldn't focus on her right now. I'd called the monster to me, and I had to figure out a way to deal with him without getting her hurt.

The sound of a door creaking, then the slow, steady footfalls heading down the stairs, caused my heart to pound against my chest. A long, thin arm reached up and pulled the string of the hanging bulb. Bright light flooded the room, causing me to squint, shifting my focus away from the predator getting closer to me.

"Hey, Dana." He swiped the hair out of my face. "I missed you."

I held back the shiver of disgust as his minty breath fanned across my face. It had taken me years to wipe away the memories of his smell and the way his voice sounded. I was face-to-face with my worst nightmare, and now, I had to make him believe I'd missed him, too.

"I missed you too, Harold." His eyes softened. "Why didn't you call me?"

With his face only inches away from mine, his eyes flitted back and forth between my eyes and lips. He leaned forward, and I knew what he wanted to do. "If you needed me, you didn't have to take Delaney," I said, and he stopped close to my lips but didn't kiss me. Thank God. "I would have come."

A mask of rage fell over his face as he backed away from me. He started pacing, his hands pulling at his hair. "You!" He pointed at me accusingly. "You were with him, and you had me locked away!"

Shit! Shit! Think, Dana. Think. Remember your training. Try to make a personal connection with him.

"You needed help back then, Harold." Hopefully, continuing to call him by his name would be personal enough. I didn't think I could go any further than that. "You hurt those other women before you met me. They wanted you to get help before we could be together. Even your doctor said it was best."

"You spoke to Dr. Stephens?"

"I did, Harold. He said that it was the best way if I wanted to be with you. That's why I went along with everything they said. I testified so we could be together."

He stopped pacing. "You wanted to be with me if I got help?"

"Of course I did, but now, if you want us to be together, you have to let Delaney go. They're not going to let us be together if you hurt her."

"No, no, no, no." He started pacing again, frantically shaking his head. "She'll tell that we took her, and then they will take us away again. Four will not like it if we have to go away again. They didn't like the hospital."

Four?

"I promise they won't, Harold. There's nothing for you and *Four* to be afraid of, but if you want us to be together, you have to let her go."

Damn, I hoped this worked. Even if I didn't get out of here, at least Delaney would be safe. I wasn't giving up on myself getting out of here just yet, but right now, Delaney was my priority.

"Okay," he said, sighing.

"Okay?" I asked, shocked but making sure he really had agreed to let her go.

"Yes, I will let her go just for you, but if she tells anyone where we're at, I'll kill her entire family, including that cute little girl of hers. What's her name again?"

He snapped his fingers and walked over to Delaney. I couldn't see the fear in her eyes, but I knew it was there. I'd been there before. This man was unstable, and I believed every threat he made. His body count had already surpassed ten innocent women.

"That's right. Her name is Amara, right? She's beautiful, by the way. Around the age of my daughter."

"You have a daughter?" I asked, surprised.

"I had a daughter," he corrected, moving his attention back to me and away from Delaney, which was what I wanted. "Her mother was one of the first bodies I delivered to Detective LaCroix."

My surprise and horror must have been written all over my face because a smile crossed his. "No, I didn't kill my daughter, Dana. But her mother was a bitch and a temporary replacement until we got back together."

"Please let Delaney go, Harold," I said, trying to get him back on track, but his brows furrowed after he eyed the small window across the room. I didn't know what he saw there, but I had to keep him focused. The shift in his mood covered the room. Anger poured from him, and his breathing picked up. His face turned red.

His calloused hands circled my neck as he straddled my body. He moved quicker than I expected, but there wasn't anything I could do. The natural fibers of the rope had already cut into my skin, blood covering my wrists. The pressure from the rope and his hands was too much. My eyes widened, and his filled with lust while the bulge in his pants grew against my body. Tears streamed down my cheeks as I watched the man of my nightmares take pleasure in taking my life.

Delaney screamed, but it did nothing to stop him. His grip tightened as glee covered his face.

"I love you, Dana," Harold whispered as black dots danced in my eyes. "For eternity. In this life and the next."

It wouldn't be long now. My lungs burned as I tried to pull air into them. My eyes stung as blood vessels burst. This was my last day on this earth, and regrets filled my thoughts. I regretted that so many had to die because of me, and I hoped the families could one day forgive me. And I regretted not seeing Rey one last time. I hoped he could forgive me for leaving again.

Delaney's screams faded as the darkness seeped in. Someone else yelled from a distance, but I couldn't keep my eyes open any longer. The darkness had finally won.

CHAPTER FOURTEEN

DETECTIVE REY LACROIX

As soon as Agent Hart moved down the steps and announced himself, I saw red. It took all of two seconds to empty my magazine into the back of Harold Greely as he straddled my wife, his hands around her neck.

Of course, I'd catch shit for shooting a suspect in the back, but I'd face the consequences like a fucking trooper as long as Dana survived.

I ignored the body on the floor and focused on Dana. She wasn't breathing, so I started CPR, hoping I could save her. Her face was covered in Greely's blood, but I couldn't focus on that right now. Agent Hart had pulled off his jacket to cover Delaney after cutting her loose and then escorting her out of the building. Amir had gone to the other address with the other team. Hopefully, he'd get word we'd found them. One of the other agents who'd entered the home with us covered Dana and cut the rope binding her while I tried to bring her back.

"Come on, sweetheart," I said as I continued to give her breaths and chest compressions. "Stay with me."

"The ambulance is two minutes out," Agent Hart called out, but I continued to focus on her until someone pulled me away and took over.

"Let me help her!" I yelled, but some of the other agents pushed me farther away until they eventually dragged me out of the house altogether.

• • • • • • • • •

"Rey, you need to go home." Delaney squeezed my shoulder. I didn't even hear her walk in. "Don't you have your interview with Internal Affairs today?"

I groaned. Just thinking about it pissed me off. I was being questioned about my actions on the day I killed Harold Greely. I'd known it was coming, but I'd hoped they would give me a little leeway since Dana was still unconscious in the hospital. My interview with Internal Affairs was the last thing on my mind. I'd been in a trance, staring at Dana, hoping and praying she'd wake up. I wasn't a religious man, but I prayed to whoever would listen. To whoever would grant me favor to bring her back to me. So far, nothing had worked, but I hadn't given up.

It had been six days since I'd been sitting at her bedside, scared she'd wake up while I wasn't here or die while I wasn't here. Either way, this small room had become my home away from home. Delaney had been bringing me food and clothes since Dana had been admitted because she worked here.

"I'll sit with her until you get back."

"I can't leave her."

The only time I left her side was to use the bathroom, and it was only because I had to because my place was next to her.

"I destroyed our lives all those years ago. I'll be damned if I let her think I've turned my back on her again."

"Rey..."

"I've been so lost without her, Delaney." I placed my hand on top of Dana's and dropped my head against it. "What if she doesn't make it?"

"You can't think like that, Rey," Delaney said.

"I fucked up. I let this happen. She warned me about Chanel, and I couldn't see it for what it was. I thought she was just jealous of someone I'd fucked. How in the hell could I've been so stupid?"

"Me? Jealous?"

Her raspy voice caused me to break. I sobbed like a baby while she ran her hands through my hair.

"I'm going to go get the doctor," Delaney said, excusing herself while I had a breakdown.

After I calmed down, wiping my eyes, the only thing I could do was stare into the beautiful brown eyes of the woman who'd stolen my heart all those years ago. The woman I'd die for. The woman I was stupid enough to let get away.

I stood and wiped away the tears trickling down her cheeks. "Is he dead?"

"Yes."

She released a sigh of relief, then sadness filtered into her eyes. "I didn't think you would get to me in time."

I sat on the edge of the bed, trying to get as close to her as possible.

"You're mine, Dana LaCroix. I may have been an ass these past few years, but that much hasn't changed. I'll do anything for you."

Her eyes softened. "I know, Rey. I'm just glad he can't hurt anyone else."

"Me too." I kissed her forehead. "You get some sleep. You need your rest."

"You have to leave?" she asked.

"I do, but I'll be back before you know it. I love you."

A faint smile crossed her lips. "I love you too, Rey."

When her gentle snores filtered into my ears, I was more at peace than I'd been in years. The woman I loved was a survivor. Years ago, one drink changed the course of her life, putting her on the path to greatness. Now, it was my turn to support everything she wanted and to be the husband she needed me to be. Things would be different now. I'd do everything in my power to make things easier for her until the day I died.

Chapter Fifteen

Epilogue

"Dr. LaCroix, Mr. Steele would like to see you in the conference room immediately," my assistant, Renee, said. I looked up from the mountain of paperwork I'd been sifting through since I arrived this morning.

"Did he say why?" I asked.

After the Infinity Killer, or Harold Greely, as I knew him, was killed, the Bureau had demanded I take at least six weeks off before returning to work, not including the week and a half I'd spent in the hospital. Now, two months after the end of my official vacation, I'd returned to a load of cases that needed to be separated so I could tackle the highest-priority files first.

"No, ma'am. He didn't say."

"Thank you."

I closed the file, exited my office behind her, and made my way to the conference room. Like any other time he was expecting me, I walked in without knocking. When I entered the room, all the men rose. I was shocked to see Rey beside Mr. Steele at the head of the conference table. My brows drew together, and he winked. He hadn't said anything to me this morning about needing the FBI's help with a case.

"Dr. LaCroix, I'm glad you could join us on such short notice, but your husband insisted that you be brought in on this case the Atlanta PD is asking the FBI's help with."

After everything, Rey had insisted that we no longer be apart. Wherever I was, that was where he wanted to be. So, we'd had a lengthy conversation about where we wanted our relationship to go. He'd wanted to get remarried. I had wanted the same thing, but we still had the same issue. I wasn't giving up my job. If he wanted to be with me, he'd have to move to Atlanta. I had expected a fight. Louisiana was Rey's home. He absolutely loved his job, but to my surprise, he'd had no problem putting in a transfer this time.

After the shooting, Internal Affairs cleared him of any wrongdoing in Harold Greely's death. He'd received the highest honor given to a law enforcement officer by the Governor of Louisiana for his work to bring justice to Greely's victims.

Now, he was a detective in the Atlanta PD. I wondered what case was so important that he needed to bring in the FBI, specifically me. It had to be bad.

I took the seat beside Rey and next to Mr. Steele. "I'm happy to help if I can."

All the men returned to their seats.

"Detective LaCroix, you have the floor."

Rey rose from his seat and made his way to the front of the conference table. I admired him as his muscles shifted under his gray polo and khakis. Today, his shoulder-length hair was pulled into a loose bun on the back of his head, his gun was latched at his hip, and his badge hung from a chain around his neck.

Assembled on one side of the table was Mr. Steele, myself, Agent Hoffman—who still looked like he would rather eat shit than be in the same room with me—Agent Johnathan Grant, and Aaron. While I was missing, Aaron and Rey had worked together to find me and Delaney, but anytime I was around him, it was still awkward as hell. For me, at least.

The longing for what we shared still lingered in his eyes, but I think he understood I had moved on. Nothing would ever happen between us again. Rey and I were together, and he had come to terms with the fact that Aaron would always be around as long as I worked for the FBI.

"We received an anonymous tip of a body in an abandoned house. Once we got there, we found a female, late teens to early twenties, chained to the wall in one of the rooms."

"Okay, but what do you need the FBI's help with?" Agent Grant asked. "Bodies are a common occurrence in Atlanta."

"That may be true, but above the head of the woman was a symbol drawn in the blood," Rey said. "I've seen the symbol before, and I'm going to assume before testing is done on the blood that it's the victim's."

He slid a picture across the table, and Agent Grant looked at it before passing it around the table. When it reached me, I looked at it and raised my brows in surprise.

"Rey, is this what I think it is?"

"I hate to say it, but it is."

"Okay, someone needs to start explaining," Mr. Steele said, looking between Rey and me.

"About five years ago, my department in the parish got an anonymous tip of a body in an abandoned boathouse located in one of the bayous," Rey said. "Sixteen-year-old Christine Wallace had been chained to the wall with a symbol written in blood above her head. The symbol was the alchemist's symbol for arsenic. That symbol." He pointed to the photograph. "It was later determined the killer used Christine's blood to draw the symbol. I uncovered over seventy murders across the country that can be attributed to this one killer."

"You've got to be fucking kidding me," Mr. Steele said, running his hand through his hair.

"I wish I was," Rey said. "At least three in Louisiana, and now this one in Atlanta. The more I dig, I don't think this will be the only one I find here or across the state."

"We could never figure out a definite pattern to his movements," Rey continued, "but all the victims were females, late teens, early twenties, and different demographics. To me, all the victims seemed random."

"Nothing's random," I said.

"That's what you told me back then, too," he said with a smile. "I'm requesting the FBI's help, specifically this team, as well as Dana."

"And why this team?" Mr. Steele asked, and I wondered the same thing.

"When Dana was taken, I saw how well these men worked together to get her back. I need that kind of help."

"And I assume since you've requested that she be here for this meeting, you would like her to give you insights on this killer?"

"Yes, sir," Rey replied. "She's used to helping me out, but I think with this level of brutality and the sheer number of victims, the FBI has resources the Atlanta PD doesn't have."

Rey's phone rang, and his brows furrowed at the caller ID. "I need to take this."

While Rey took his phone call, I picked up the picture of the crime scene. A young Caucasian woman had iron cuffs attached to each wrist, which had been chained to steel rings bolted to the wall. Her head hung loosely, and her uneven, dirty hair hung haphazardly down to her shoulders. My eyes zeroed in on her fingernails as well as her toes. Although dirty and chipped, both had been professionally done.

She, at least, has enough money to get manicures and pedicures, or someone pays for them. And iron cuffs. Who the hell has iron cuffs, and where can you get them?

"We received another call," Rey said, breaking into my thoughts. "Another body is said to be two blocks from where we found this one."

Mr. Steele sighed. "You got your team, Detective LaCroix, but the FBI takes the lead."

About Author

Courtney Dean is a wife and mother of two boys from North Carolina. She holds a BA in History w/American History and a MA in History w/Public History. When not writing she enjoys researching family history, reading dark romance, and hanging out with her family.

Acknowledgments

MC ROMANCE

DEMONS UNITED MC SERIES
DEMON'S SAVIOR
DEMON'S WAR
DEMON'S END

NOMAD: DEMONS UNITED MC (Standalone)

SIN CITY MC
GRIMM

Saint: Sin City MC Oakland Chapter Vella
MAFIA ROMANCE

SOUTHIE

VINCENZO'S PROMISE
PARANORMAL ROMANCE

THE ROYAL BLOODLINES SERIES
THE WITCH WHO WILL BE QUEEN
THE SEER'S DESTINY

GIRL'S OF MIGHT AND MAGIC: ANTHOLOGY BY DIVERSE
BOOKS WITH MAGIC
R

Also By Courtney Dean

MC ROMANCE

DEMONS UNITED MC SERIES
DEMON'S SAVIOR

DEMON'S WAR

DEMON'S END

NOMAD: DEMONS UNITED MC (Standalone)

SIN CITY MC
GRIMM

SAINT: Sin City MC (Oakland Chapter)
MAFIA ROMANCE

SOUTHIE

VINCENZO'S PROMISE
PARANORMAL ROMANCE

THE ROYAL BLOODLINES SERIES

THE WITCH WHO WILL BE QUEEN

THE SEER'S DESTINY

GIRL'S OF MIGHT AND MAGIC: ANTHOLOGY BY DIVERSE

BOOKS WITH MAGIC

<u>ROMANTIC SUSPENSE</u>

BLOOD AND SAND: THE LACROIX MYSTERIES